I0651401

Mary Mapes Dodge

The Land of Pluck

Stories and Sketches for Young Folk

Mary Mapes Dodge

The Land of Pluck
Stories and Sketches for Young Folk

ISBN/EAN: 9783744769327

Printed in Europe, USA, Canada, Australia, Japan

Cover: Foto ©Andreas Hilbeck / pixelio.de

More available books at **www.hansebooks.com**

THE LAND OF PLUCK

Other Books by
Mary Mapes Dodge

♣

DONALD AND DOROTHY.

HANS BRINKER.

THEOPHILUS AND OTHERS.

ALONG THE WAY.

RHYMES AND JINGLES.

WHEN LIFE IS YOUNG,

ETC., ETC., ETC.

TWO BOYS OF HOLLAND.
[From an old Dutch painting.]

THE LAND OF PLUCK

STORIES AND SKETCHES
FOR YOUNG FOLK

BY

MARY MAPES DODGE

AUTHOR OF "HANS BRINKER"
"DONALD AND DOROTHY"
"RHYMES AND JINGLES"
ETC., ETC.

NEW YORK
THE CENTURY CO.
1894

Copyright, 1894, by
THE CENTURY CO.

THE DE VINNE PRESS.

AUTHOR'S NOTE

The paper on Holland which constitutes Part I of this book has now been expanded to more than double the proportions of "The Land of Pluck" as printed a few years ago in "St. Nicholas."

The stories and sketches composing Part II are here for the first time collected in book form.

The frontispiece "Two Boys of Holland" has been engraved from a fine Dutch painting, attributed to Cuyp, and owned by Mr. Charles T. Barney of New York, who courteously allowed it to be copied for use in this volume.

CONTENTS

THE LAND OF PLUCK

THE LAND of PLUCK

CHAPTER I

ON BOTH SIDES OF THE DIKE

FAR over the sea is a famous little country generally known as Holland; but that name, even if it should mean Hollow land, or How land? does not describe it half so well as this—The Little Land of Pluck.

Verily, a queerer bit of earth was never shone upon by the sun nor washed by the tide. It is the oddest, funniest country that ever raised its head from the waves (and, between ourselves, it does not quite do that), the most topsyturvy landscape, the most amphibious spot in the universe,—as the Man in the Moon cannot deny,—the chosen butt of the elements, and good-naturedly the laughing-stock of mankind. Its people are the queerest and drollest of all the nations; and yet so plucky, so wise and resolute and strong, that "beating the Dutch" has become a familiar byword for expressing the limits of mortal performance.

As for the country, for centuries it was not exactly anywhere; at least it objected to remaining just the same for any length of time, in any one place. It may be said to have lain around loose on the waters of a certain portion of Europe, playing peek-a-boo with its inhabitants; now coming to the surface here and there to attend to matters, then taking a dive for change of scene,—and a most disastrous dive it often proved.

Rip Van Winkle himself changed less between his great sleeping and waking than Holland has altered many a time, between sunset and dawn. All its firmness and permanence seems to have been soaked out of it, or rather to have filtered from the land into the people. Every field hesitates whether to turn into a pond or not, and the ponds always are trying to leave the country by the shortest cut. One would suppose that under this condition of things the only untroubled creatures would be turtles and ducks; but no, strangest and most mysterious of all, every living thing in Holland appears to be thoroughly placid and content! The Dutch mind, so to speak, is at once anti-dry and waterproof. Little children run about in fields where once their grandfathers sailed over the billows; and youths and maidens row their pleasure-boats where their ancestors played "tag" among the haystacks. When the tide sweeps unceremoniously over Mynheer's garden, he lights his pipe, takes his fishing-rod, and sits down on his back porch to try his luck. If his pet pond breaks loose and slips away, he whistles, puts up a dam so that it cannot come back, and decides upon the crop to be raised in its place. None but the Dutch could live so tranquilly in Holland; though, for that matter, if

"MYNHEER SITS DOWN ON HIS BACK PORCH TO TRY HIS LUCK."

it had not been for the Dutch, we may be sure that by this time there would be no Holland at all.

And yet this very Holland, besides holding its own place, has managed to gain a foothold on almost every

quarter of the globe. An account of its colonies is a
history in itself. In the East Indies alone it has under
its authority more than thirty million people.

It is said that the Greenlanders, in spite of the discom-
forts of their country, become so very fond of it that even
the extreme cold is considered a luxury.
In some such way, I suppose, the Hollander becomes infatuated with water.
He deems no landscape, no pleasure-
spot complete without it. It is
funny to see the artificial pond
that a Dutchman will have beneath his very window; and
funny, also, to see how soon the
pond will try to look like land,
by filming itself over with a coat
of green. Many of the city people have little summer-houses,
or pavilions, near the outskirts
of the town. They are built
just large enough for the
family to sit in. Each
zomerhuis, as it is called,
is sure to be surrounded
by a ditch, if indeed it is not built out over the water.
Its chief ornaments are its little bridges, its fanciful roof,
and its Dutch motto painted over the entrance. Hither
the family repair on summer afternoons. Mynheer sips
his coffee, smokes his pipe, and gazes at the water. His
vrouw knits or sews; and the children fish from the win-

dows, or climb the little bridges, or paddle about in skiffs, gathering yellow water-lilies. Near by, perhaps, they can hear some bargeman's wife singing her cheery song while busy at her housekeeping, or rather homekeeping, for she lives on the canal-boat. That is her flower-garden growing on a corner of the deck, quite unconscious that it is doing anything remarkable in blooming over the water. In fact, it is in much less danger of sinking there than it would be on shore.

Now, these oddities arise mainly from the fact that though mankind cannot help admiring this Land of Pluck, the ocean has always looked down upon it. A large portion of Holland lies below the level of the sea,—in some places as much as twenty or thirty feet. Besides, the country abounds with lakes and rivers that persist in swelling and choking and overflowing to such a degree that, as I said before, none but the Dutch could do anything with them. All this disturbs an unpleasant phantom named Fog, who has a cousin in London. He sometimes rises like a great smoke over the land, shutting out the sunlight, and wrapping everything and everybody in a veil of mist, so that it is almost as much as a person's life is worth to venture out of doors, for fear of tumbling into a canal. Again, the greater part of Holland is so flat that the wind sweeps across it in every direction, putting the waters up to no little mischief, and blowing about all the dry sand it can find, heaping it, scattering it, in the wildest possible way.

What wonder the Dutch have always been wise, plucky, and strong? They have had to struggle for a foothold

1*

upon the very land of their birth. They have had to push
back the ocean to prevent it from rolling in upon them.
They have had to wall in the rivers and lakes to keep
them within bounds. They have been forced to decide
which should be land and which should be water,—
forever digging, building, embanking, and pumping for
dear existence. They had no stones, no timber, that
they had not themselves procured from elsewhere.
Added to this, they have had the loose, blowing sand
in their mind's eye for ages; never forgetting it, gov-
erning its drifts, and where its vast, silent heapings (as
in the great dunes along the coast) have proved useful as a protection, they have planted sea-bent and
other vegetation to fasten it in its place. Even the riotous
wind has been made their slave. Caught by thousands of
long-armed windmills, it does their grinding, pumping,
draining, sawing. When it ceases to blow, those great
white sleeve-like sails all over the country hang limp and
listless in the misty air, or are tucked trimly out of sight;
but let the first breath of a gale be felt, and straightway,
with one flutter of preparation, every arm is turning slowly,
steadily, with a peculiar plenty-of-time air, or is whirling
as if the spirit of seventy Dutchmen had taken possession of it.

You scarcely can stand anywhere in Holland without
seeing from one to twenty windmills. Many of them are
built in the form of a two-story tower, the second story
being smaller than the first, with a balcony at its base
from which it tapers upward until the cap-like top is
reached. High up, near the roof, the great axis juts from

ONE OF THE WINDMILLS.

the wall; and to this are fastened two prodigious arms,
formed somewhat like ladders, bearing great sheets of canvas, whose business it is to catch the mischief-maker and
set him at work. These mills stand like huge giants
guarding the country. Their bodies are generally of a
dark red; and their heads, or roofs, are made to turn this
way and that, according to the direction of the wind.
Their round eye-window is always staring. Altogether,
they seem to be keeping a vigilant watch in every direc-

tion. Sometimes they stand clustered together; sometimes alone, like silent sentinels; sometimes in long rows,
like ranks of soldiers. You see them rising from the
midst of factory buildings, by the cottages, on the polders
(the polders are lakes pumped dry and turned into farms);
on the wharves; by the rivers; along the canals; on the
dikes; in the cities — everywhere! Holland would n't

"ALONG THE CANAL."

be Holland without its windmills, any more than it would
be Holland without its dikes and its Dutchmen.

A certain zealous dame is said to have once attempted
to sweep the ocean away with a broom. The Dutch have
been wiser than she. They are a slow and deliberate people.
Desperation may use brooms, but deliberation prefers clay
and solid masonry. So, slowly and deliberately, the dikes,
those great walls of cement and stone, have risen to
breast the buffeting waves. And the queer part of it is,

A DUTCH DIKE AS SEEN FROM THE LAND SIDE.

they are so skilfully slanted and paved on the outside
with flat stones that the efforts of the thumping waves
to beat them down only make them all the firmer!

These Holland dikes are among the wonders of the
world. I cannot say for how many miles they stretch
along the coast, and throughout the interior; but you may
be sure that wherever a dike is necessary to keep back
the encroaching waters, there it is. Otherwise, nothing
would be there—at least, nothing in the form of land;
nothing but a fearful illustration of the principal law of
hydrostatics: Water always seeks its level.

Sometimes the dikes, however carefully builded, will
spring a leak, and if this be not promptly attended to, terrible results are sure to follow. In threatened places guards
are stationed at intervals, and a steady watch is kept up
night and day. At the first signal of danger, every Dutchman
within hearing of the startling bell is ready to rush to the
rescue. When the weak spot is discovered, what do you
think is used to meet the emergency? What, but straw—
everywhere else considered the most helpless of all things

in water! Yet straw, in the hands of the Dutch, has a will of its own. Woven into huge mats and securely pressed against the embankment, it defies even a rushing tide, eager to sweep over the country.

These dikes form almost the only perfectly dry land to be seen from the ocean-side. They are high and wide, with fine carriage-roads on top, sometimes lined with buildings, windmills, and trees. On one side of them, and nearly on a level with the edge, is the sea, lake, canal, or river, as the case may be; on the other, the flat fields stretching damply along at their base. Cottage roofs, therefore, may be lower than the shining line of the water; frogs squatting on the shore can take quite a bird's-eye view of the landscape; and little fish wriggle their tails higher than the tops of the willows near by. Horses look complacently down upon the bell-towers; and men in skiffs and canal-boats cannot know when they are passing Dirk's cottage close by, except by seeing the smoke from its chimney,—or perhaps the cart-wheel that he has perched upon the peak of its overhanging thatched roof, in the hope that some stork will build her nest there, and so bring him good luck.

A butterfly may take quite an upward flight in Holland, leaving flowers and shrubs and trees beneath her, and, after all, mount only to where a snail is sunning himself on the water's edge; or a toad may take a reckless leap from the land side of the dike, and, alighting on a tree-top, be obliged to reach earth in monkey-fashion, by leaping from branch to branch!

CHAPTER II

TO the birds, skimming high over the country, it must be a fanciful sight—this Holland. There are the fertile farms or polders, studded with cattle and bright red cottages; shortwaisted men, women, and children, moving about in wide jackets and big wooden shoes; trees everywhere clipped into fantastical shapes, with their trunks colored white, yellow, or brick red; country mansions too, and farm-houses gaudy with roofs of brightly tinted tiles. These tiles are made of a kind of glazed earthenware, and make one feel as if all the pie-dishes in the country were lapped in rows on top of the buildings. Then the great slanting dikes, with their waters held up as if to catch the blue of the sky; the ditches, canals, and rivers trailing their shining lengths in every direction; shining lines of railway, too, that now connect most of the principal points of the Netherlands; then, the thousands of bridges, little and big; the sluice-gates, canal-locks, and windmills; the silver and golden weathercocks perched on one foot, and twitching right and left to show their contempt for the

11

wind.   All this, as you must know, makes the sun jeweler-
in-chief to the landscape, which shines and glitters and
trembles with motion and light.   Yet that is only one
way of looking at it.   A low-spirited bird might still see

CAPSIZING !

only marshes and puddles, though he might learn a good
lesson or two in seeing jolly Dutch folk, young and old,
making merry over every-day affairs.   Or one of the prac-
tical every-day sort might notice only commonplace things
— such as the country roads paved with yellow bricks;
cabbage-plots scarcely greener than the ponds nestling
everywhere among the reeds; cottages, with roofs ever so

much too big for them, perched upon wooden legs to keep them from sinking in the marsh; and horses wearing wide, stool-like shoes for the same reason. Or they might watch the wagons bumping along with drivers sitting outside, kicking the funny little crooked pole; or horses yoked three abreast, dragging obstinate loads; or women and boys harnessed to long towing-ropes, meekly drawing their loads of market-stuff up and down the canal.

Then there are the boats, large and small, of every possible Dutch style; wonderful ships made to breast the rough seas of the coast; fishing-smacks (*smakschepen*), heavy with fresh catches; the round-sterned craft by the cities, with their gilded prows and gaily painted sides; *trekschuiten*, or water-omnibuses, plying up and down the canals for the conveyance of passengers; brown-sailed *pakschuiten*, or water-carts, for carrying coal and merchandise upon these same water-roads; barges loaded

A WATER OMNIBUS.

with peat; pleasure-boats with their showy sails; the
little skiffs, the rafts, the chip boats launched by white-
haired urchins kneeling in the mud.

OVER THE CHIMNEYS AND HOUSE-TOPS (AMSTERDAM).

Then, mingling confusedly with masts, and windmills,
and sails are the long rows of willows, firs, beeches, or
elms, planted on the highways wherever root-hold can be
found or manufactured; the stiff, symmetrical gardens,
with their nodding tulips and brilliant shrubs; the great
white storks flying to and fro with outstretched necks
and legs, busily attending to family needs, or settling upon
the quaint gabled roofs, perhaps, of Amsterdam; water-fowl

dipping with soft splashings into the tide ; rabbits scudding here and there ; water-rats slyly slipping into their crannies, and bright water-insects rocking at the surface on reed and tangleweed. Seeing all this, our birds have not seen half ; but they have ample time to look, for bird-life is not the uncertain thing in Holland that it is here. They are citizens loved and respected, and protected by rigorous laws. Stones are not thrown at their heads, nor is " salt sprinkled upon their tails." They are not afraid of guns, for the law has its eye on the gunners ; and, strangest of all, they see nothing terrible in small boys ! Young eyes, to be sure, often peep into their nests ; but the owners have been taught not to rob nor molest. Human mothers and bird mothers are in secret league. Indeed, the softest, warmest nest is not softer nor warmer than the Dutch heart has proved itself to the birds.

MYNHEER ON HIS WAY TO BUSINESS.

CHAPTER III

WHEN the coldest days of winter come, and the little songsters—and their greedy cousins, the storks—have flown away in search of warmer climes, the country still is in a glitter, for its waters are frozen. Then all Holland puts on its skates, and gets atop of its beloved water, in which before it has only dabbled. Everybody, young and old, little and big, goes skimming and sliding along the canals, over the lakes, and on the rivers.

The entire country seems one vast skating-rink. No need of red balls to tell the people that everything is ready for the sport. They know that, in their land, a cold winter means ice,—and good solid ice, too,—sometimes for weeks together. Then come out the skaters; and the sleighs; and the happy, sliding-chair folk who are pushed swiftly over the ice by friends, or by liveried lackeys, gliding close behind. Then appear,—swiftest, most dazzling of all,—the ice-boats, perhaps with merry loads of laughing boys and singing school-children. Listening to these sweet choruses, as they suddenly burst upon you and then as suddenly die away with the vanishing boat, you feel that not the wind but the joyous music fills the sails skimming so swiftly over the ice.

As you may well believe, these flying, whizzing iceboats always get the right of way, for nobody would willingly come into collision with them. They seem to

THE ICE-BOATS ARE OUT!

know that their season is brief, at the best, and they make speed while the ice shines.

Now, there is a new sensation among the pleasure-seekers. Distant shouts of men are heard, and faint crashing sounds slowly growing louder. The *ijsbrekers* are out! These, as you may guess by trying to pronounce the word, are provided with pikes for clearing a way through the ice, so that barges and other vessels may pass. Sometimes they are rather small affairs, worked by hand, and sometimes are large and heavy, and drawn by as many as

twenty or even thirty horses. There is no little excitement among the boys and girls when a big ice-breaker
comes out for the first time in the season. The great
crashing thing inspires them with wonder and admiration;
yet with all its power it cuts only a narrow pathway for
the boats. The main face of the country belongs to the
skaters.

For miles and miles the glassy ice spreads its mirror
under the blinking and dazzled sun. Everywhere is one
shining network of slippery highway. Who would walk
or ride then? Not one. Doctors skate to their patients;
clergymen to their parishioners; marketwomen to town
with baskets upon their heads. Laborers go skimming by,
with tools on their shoulders; and tradespeople, busily
planning the day's affairs; fat old burgomasters, too, with
gold-headed canes cautiously flourished to keep them in
balance; laughing girls with arms entwined; long files of
young men, shouting as they pass; children with school-
satchels slung over their shoulders,—all whizzing by, this
way and that, until you can see nothing but the flashing
of skates, and a rushing confusion of color.

And while all this is happening in the open air, the
simple indoor life is steadily going on, in the homes, the
shops, the churches, the schools, the workshops, the
picture-galleries.

Ah, the picture-galleries! All Hollanders, from the very
richest and most cultivated to almost the very humblest,
visit and enjoy the rare collections of paintings that en-
noble their principal towns and cities. And what pictures
those old Dutchmen have painted! The Dutchmen of to-

day well may be proud of them. There was Rembrandt Van Ryn (of the Rhine), perhaps the greatest portrait-painter this world has ever known; and Franz Hals and Van der Helst and Van Ostade, and the careful Gerard Dou, and Mieris and the two Cuyps, father and son, and Teniers and Adriaen Hanneman, and other great paint-ers by the score. You must read about them, and some day see their pictures, if indeed you have not already come upon them either in your books or on your travels.

But if you visit no other, you surely must plan some day to go to the Ryks Museum at Amsterdam, and see its collection of priceless Rembrandts and other treasures of Dutch art.

If you go to Holland in summer and look at the people, you will wonder when all the work was done, and who did it. The country folk move so slowly and serenely, looking as if to smoke their pipes were quite as much as they care to do,—they have so little to say, and seem to see you only because their eyes happen to be open. You feel sure if by any accident the lids dropped they would not be lifted again in a hurry. Yet there are the dikes, the water-roads, the great ship-canals, the fine old towns, the magnificent cities, the colleges, the galleries, the charit-able institutions, the churches. There are the public parks, the beautiful country-seats, the immense factories, the herring-packeries, the docks, the shipping-yards, the railways, and the telegraphs. Surely these Hollanders must work in their sleep!

But though the men outside of Amsterdam and the large cities may screen themselves with a mask of dull-

REMBRANDT'S PORTRAIT OF HIMSELF.

2*

ness, it is not so with the women. They are as lively as one could wish, taller in proportion than the men, with fresh, rosy faces, and hair that matches the sunshine. Many of them are elegant and graceful. As for work,—well, if there could be such a thing as a Dutch Barnum, he would make his fortune by exhibiting a lazy Dutchwoman—if he could find one! Ah! how they work!—brushing, mopping, scrubbing, and polishing. Judging from some houses that I have seen in Holland, I do believe the tiniest Lilliputian that Gulliver ever saw could not fill his pockets with dust if he searched through dozens of Dutch homes.

A PRETTY HOLLANDER.

Broek, a little village near beautiful Amsterdam, that city of ninety islands, is said to be the cleanest place in the world. It used to be quite famous for its North-Holland peculiarities—and even to-day it has strong characteristics of its own. It is inhabited mainly by retired Dutch merchants and their families, who seem determined to enjoy the world as it appears when scrubbed to a polish. Every morning the village shines forth as fresh as if it had just taken a bath. The wooden houses are as bright and gay as paint can make them. Their shining tiled roofs and polished facings flash up a defiance to the sun to find a speck of dust upon them. Certain dooryards, curiously paved with shells and stones, look like enormous mosaic brooches pinned to the earth ; the little canals and ditches, instead of crawling sluggishly as many of their kindred do, flow with a limpid cleanliness; the streets of fine yellow brick are carefully sanded. Even the children walk as if they were trying to make their wooden shoes express a due respect for sand and pebbles. Horses and wheeled vehicles of any kind are not allowed within the borders of the town. The pea-green window-shutters usually are closed; and the main entrances of cottages never are opened except on the occasion of a christening, a wedding, or a funeral, or when the dazzling brass knobs and knockers are to be rendered more dazzling still.

The gardens are as trim and complete as the houses; but in summer the flower-beds, all laid out in little patches, are bright with audacious blossoms nodding saucily to the prim box-border that incloses them. Most of you have seen the stocky, thick-stemmed box-plant, with its dense growth of dark, glossy little leaves. Every old-fashioned country-place in our own Middle States has had its box-bordered flower-beds, with occasional taller clumps of the shrub, looking like dumpy little trees. Well, the box-plants in Broek grow in a similar way, but they are very old, and the work of trimming and shaping their hedges

PORTRAIT OF A BOY, BY ADRIAEN HANNEMAN (BORN 1610, DIED 1666).

may have been handed down from father to son for gener-
ations. Nearly every garden in Brock has its *zomerhuis*
and its pond. Some of these ponds have queer automata
—or self-moving figures—upon them: sometimes a duck
that paddles about and flaps its wooden wings; sometimes a wooden sportsman standing upon the shore, jerkily
taking aim at the duck, but never quite succeeding in
getting his range accurate enough to warrant firing; and
sometimes a dog stands among the shrubbery and snaps
his jaws quite fiercely when he is not too damp to work.
Queer things, too, are seen in the growing box, which is
trimmed so as to fail in resembling peacocks and wolves.
Altogether, Brock is a very remarkable place. The
dairy-ly inclined inhabitants regard their kine as friends
and fellow-lodgers, and so the very cattle there live in
fine style. Pet cows, it is said, sometimes rejoice in
pretty blue ribbons tied to their tails,—and in winter
they not uncommonly find themselves daintily housed
beneath the family roof.

In some Dutch houses the rooms are covered with two
or three carpets, laid one over the other, and others have
no carpets at all, but the floors are polished, or perhaps
made of tiles laid in regular patterns. Sometimes doors
are curtained like the windows, and the beds are nearly
concealed by heavy draperies. Many among the poorer
classes sleep in rough boxes, or on shelves fixed in recesses
against the wall; so that sometimes the best bed in the
cottage looks more like a cupboard than anything else.

Whether having so much water about suggested the
idea or not, I cannot say, but certain it is that big blocks

of imported cork are quite in fashion for footstools. They stand one on each side of the great open fireplace, as though the household intended to have at least a couple of life-preservers on hand, in case of a general flood. The large earthen cup, or fire-pot, that you may see standing near, filled with burning peat, and casting a bright glow over the Dutch sentence inscribed on the tiles arching the fireplace, is very useful for warming the room on chilly days, when it is not quite cold enough for a fire. For that matter, it is a general custom in Holland to use little tin fire-boxes (with a handle, and with holes in the top lid) for warming the feet. Our Dutch ancestors brought some of them over to America long ago, and many grown-up New-Yorkers can remember seeing similar ones in use. In Holland every lady has her *voet stoof*, or foot-stove. Churches are provided with a large number; and on Sunday, boys and sometimes old women, bearing high piles of them, move softly about, distributing them among the congregation.

A DUTCH FOOT-STOVE.

CHAPTER IV

STREETS AND BYWAYS

NLY an hour's ride on the railroad from Broek to Amsterdam—and yet how different are the two! Here, as in the other large Dutch cities, you see a brisk business look on the men's faces. They are slighter in build than the rustic folk; and, not having such broad backs and short legs, not wearing leather breeches and wide jackets and big waist-buckles as the countrymen do, they quite make you forget that they are Dutch. In fact they look like New-Yorkers. Nowadays, the fashions and the stiff masculine costume of Paris and London tend to make nearly all city folk of the Christian world look alike.

Still, often in Dutch cities you see something distinctive in costume,—huge coal-scuttle bonnets on the women; and wooden shoes, that clatter-clatter at every step. Some of the women and girls have their hair cropped short and wear close-fitting caps; and these caps and headdresses are seen in great variety. Some have plain gold bands over the forehead, others have gold or silver plates at the back, and some have deep folds of rich lace hanging from them. The writer once saw two young women walking together in Rotterdam, one of whom wore a fashionable French bonnet, and the other a queer head-gear with rosettes and golden "blinders" projecting on each side of her forehead. Little girls often are very charming with their sweet, bright faces, their clean, trig, simple attire, and their queer white caps decked with a gold band over the forehead and small gold twirls dangling at each side. The little visitor in the picture on page 31 is one of these, and you see how carefully she has slipped off her wooden shoes so as not to soil her hostess's spotless floors. Then there are the boys, cheerful, clean, and sturdy; some dressed in modern-looking hats and suits; but others wearing such short jackets and loose knee-breeches, you would declare they had borrowed the former from their little brothers and the latter from their grandfathers.

Now and then, in our own country, we hear vague rumors of a person having been born with a silver spoon in his mouth. As a rule, we scorn to credit such stories, but if we were told that all Dutchmen were born with pipes in their mouths, we probably should not consider it worth while to doubt. In making an inventory of a Dutch rustic's face, you would need to mention two eyes, two ears, one nose, one mouth, and one pipe. To be sure, there might be but one eye, or one ear, or no nose; but there certainly would be a pipe. The pipe-rack on the wall, and a large box of tobacco attached beneath, so that any guest

A LITTLE VISITOR.

or stranger may help himself, may frequently be seen in Dutch farm-houses. The men, and too often the boys, smoke, smoke, smoke, as if some malicious fairy had given

them a perpetual season-ticket for enjoying the privilege. Perhaps that is why they seem so sleepy; and yet, with what a sudden glow both pipe and Dutchman can brighten at a whiff!

Instead of seeming to shrivel up, inside and out, as constant smokers in other lands are apt to do, a Dutchman grows sleeker

A MAIDEN FROM MONNIKENDAM.

and fatter behind his pipe; as if the same fairy who gave him the season-ticket had perched herself invisibly on the bowl and was continually blowing him out like a rubber balloon.

All things are reversed in Holland. The main entrance to the finest public building in the country, The Palace,[1] or late town-hall, of Amsterdam, is its back door. Bashful maidens hire beaus to escort them to the Kermis, or fair, on festival-days. Timid citizens are scared in the dead of the night by their own watchmen, who at every quarter of the hour make such a noise with their wooden clappers, one would suppose the town to be on fire. You

---

[1] A noble town-hall it is, too ; but the building, to be safe and dry, has to stand on more than thirteen thousand piles driven deep into the spongy soil.

3

THE PALACE, OR TOWN-HALL, AT AMSTERDAM.

will see sleds used in summer there. They go bumping
over the bare cobblestones, while the driver holds a drip-
ping oil-rag in advance of the runners to lessen the fric-
tion. You will see streets of water; and the country
roads paved as carefully as Broadway. You will see
vessels hitched, like horses, to their owners' door-posts;
and whole rows of square-peaked houses with overlapping
stories and roofs seeming to lean over the street, just
as if they were getting ready to tumble. Instead of solemn, striking clocks, you will hear church chimes playing
snatches of operatic airs every quarter of an hour, by
way of marking the time.

You will see looking-glasses hanging outside of the
dwellings; and, occasionally, mysterious pincushions displayed on the street-doors. The first are called *spionnen*
(or *spionnetjen*), and are so arranged outside of the windows, that persons sitting inside can, without being seen,
enjoy a reflection of all that is going on in the street.
They can learn, too, what visitor may be coming, and
watch him rubbing his soles to a polish before entering.
The pincushion means that a new baby has appeared in
the household. If white or blue, the new-comer is a girl;
if red, it is a little Dutchman. Some of these signals
are very showy affairs; some are not cushions at all, but
merely shingles trimmed with ribbon or lace; and, among
the poorest class, it is not uncommon to see merely a
white or red string tied to the door-latch—fit token of
the meager life the poor little stranger is destined to lead.

Sometimes, instead of either pincushion or shingle,
you will see a large placard hung outside of the front

SOME ONE AT THE WINDOW IS WATCHING!

door. Then you may know that somebody in the house is ill, and his or her present condition is described on the placard for the benefit of inquiring friends; and sometimes, when such a placard has been taken down, you may meet a grim-looking man on the street, dressed in black tights, a short cloak, and a high hat, from which a long black streamer is flying. This is the *Aanspreker*, going from house to house to tell certain persons that their friend is dead. He attends to funerals, and bears invitations to all friends whose presence may be desired. A strange weird-looking figure he is; and he wears a peculiar, professional cast of countenance that is anything but refreshing.

Ah! here is something more cheerful! For now a little cart rattles past, drawn by a span of orderly dogs,

A STREET IN ROTTERDAM

3*

and filled with shining brass kettles that were brimming with milk when it started on its round. How nimbly the little animals trot over the stones! How promptly they heed the voice of their young master stalking leisurely along the sidew— no, not on the sidewalk, but on the narrow footpath of yellow brick that stretches along near the houses! Excepting this, the cobble pavement, if there be no canal, reaches

A YOUNG WATER-CARRIER.

entirely across the street from door to door. Occasionally one may see dogs dragging tiny fish-carts. They jog

READY FOR CUSTOMERS.

along in such practised style, we may be sure they were
taught at the dog-school in Amsterdam. But oftener, in
Holland, the small milk-cart or water-cart is drawn by
a robust boy, or a pretty rosy-cheeked girl with eyes
brighter than the shining brass water-jar she may

CARRYING MILK AND CHEESE TO MARKET.

carry. Those canal-boats around the corner, wending
their way among the houses, are loaded with peat for
the people to burn; coal is a luxury used only by the
rich. That barge by the market-place, drawn up to
the street's edge (for many of the principal thoroughfares

A WATER-BARGE.

are half water and half street), is laden with — what do
you think? What should you suppose these people would,
least of all, need to buy? You see these canals, following
and crossing the streets in every direction; you see the
mastheads and sails rising everywhere, in among the
trees and steeples, showing that river or sea always is
close at hand; you know that all Holland is a kind of
wet sponge; and the guide-books will tell you that every
house is built upon long wooden piles driven deep into the
marsh, or it could not stand there at all. Now, what do
you think these barges contain? What but water!—
water for the people to drink. It is brought for the
purpose from Utrecht, or the river Vecht, or from some
favored inland spot. All along the coast, just where Holland is wettest, our poor Dutchmen must go without any
drinking-water, for there is none fit to swallow, unless
they buy from the barges, or catch the rain almost as
soon as it falls.

NEAR SUPPER-TIME.

ON THE BEACH AT SCHEVENINGEN.

CHAPTER V

DUTCH ODDITIES

Now, is not Holland a funny land? Where else do the people pray for fish and never pray for rain? Where else do they build enormous factories for the cutting and polishing of such little things as diamonds? Where else do peasant women wear solid gold and costly old lace on their heads? Where else do persons carry foot-stoves about in their hands? Where else do crowds of folk sit on the sea-shore as at Scheveningen, every one in a great high hut-like wicker chair with a window on each side? In what other country are over eighteen hundred varieties of tulips cultivated? — tulips ranging from the palest tints to the most brilliant hues and gorgeous combinations of colors. Where else do funny wooden heads or gapers at the apothecaries' windows "make faces" for all who have to take physic? Where else is fire — in the form of red-hot peat — sold in summer by the pailful?

Is not water often as fertile as land, in Holland? Cannot the frogs there look down upon chimney-swallows? Did not the learned Erasmus, who knew how the piles were driven in, say that their city people lived like crows, on the tops of trees? And does not everybody know that "Dutch pink" is as yellow as gold?

In what other land do men cut down willow-trees to make shoes of? and where else are shoes not only worn on the feet but made to serve on occasion as improvised flower-pots, hammers, toy boats, boxes and baskets, and Christmas stockings?

These wooden shoes, or *klompen*,— well named from the noise they make upon hard roads and cobbled streets,— are of all degrees, from the huge affairs worn by heavy working-men to the dainty bits of clumsiness in which little children trudge about. The well-to-do peasant of Holland, on winter evenings, loves to carve pretty patterns upon these small klompen for the delight of his darling Jantje and Kassy. Dainty or not, the shoes must be slipped off by their wearer upon entering any tidy cottage. A row of klompen standing outside some prim doorway is no uncommon sight; and if, in addition, a pretty juffrouw [1]

[1] Pronounced *yuffrow*.

ANOTHER PAIR OF KLOMPEN EXPECTED.

DRYING SHOES BEFORE THE FIRE.

or maiden on the threshold peers expectantly up the street, one may well suspect that still another guest will soon arrive, and add his klompen to the row.

French shoe-polish is not for klompen. What they like is plenty of soap and water and a good scraping and scrubbing, inside and out, on Saturday, and a thorough drying by the fire or a bleaching in the sunshine. All Dutch folk love to be spick and span for Sunday. So, if ever you visit Holland and see a klompen-bush in full bloom, you will know that it is only the family shoes hung out to dry after their Saturday "shine,"—and, of course, a Dutch "shine" must be snowy white!

Even in their formal courtesies, the Dutch have queer ways of their own. For instance, it is said that in certain towns when, in walking along the street, they come upon the home of a friend, or a house at which they have been socially entertained, they bow in passing it—yes, bow to the house, bow to the windows, even if not a person can be seen there. And a very pretty custom it is, for it shows good feeling and kindly remembrance of hospitality enjoyed.

We are told, too, that at Kitwyk, during the morning hours —indeed, from the first breakfast of early morning to the second breakfast — a noon serving of biscuit and *koffij* (coffee)— ladies and maids do not make any attempt at fine dressing. And, strange to say, if in this

A KLOMPEN-BUSH IN BLOOM.

magic space of time, they choose to go out of doors, either about their own homes, or to the market-place, or to the great town-pump, they are supposed to be invisible! In other words, one must not recognize them nor even appear to see them, so long as they are in their clogs, crimps, nightcaps, and jackets, or wrappers,—which, it seems, constitute the forenoon undress uniform of many a Dutch lady who may shine resplendent later in the day.

And now comes the greatest oddity of all,—the Tulip Craze, or Tulipomania, as it is called, which raged over Holland early in the seventeenth century. Have you not read of it?— how the cultivating and owning of tulips seemed for a while to be the only thing men cared for? The first specimen seen in Holland came from Constantinople in 1599. The rare beauty of the flower—called tulip on account of its

THE TOWN PUMP AT KITWYK.

resemblance to a turban (*tulipa*)—at once attracted great attention. Rich Hollanders sent to Constantinople direct for the bulbs. They vied with one another in obtaining the most beautiful varieties, and in having the finest tulip-beds.   At last this taste, growing to a fancy, then to an ambition, became a mania.   The same thing would now be called "tulip on the brain."   Everybody had

"HO! HO! I THOUGHT HER LITTLE TULIP-BULB WAS AN ONION, AND I SWALLOWED IT!"

it—old, young, rich, and poor.   One rich man at Haarlem gave half of his fortune for a single root.   By the year 1635, persons were known to invest 100,000 florins[1] for thirty or forty roots.   A tulip of the species *Admiral Liefken* sold for 4400 florins.   The *Semper Augustus* easily brought 2000 florins.   And one superb specimen of the *Semper Augustus* actually sold for 13,000 florins,— or 5200 dollars.   At one time there were but two roots of this variety in Holland; one belonged to a gentleman of Haarlem, the other to a trader in Amsterdam.   Both of these were eagerly sought for by infatuated tulip-men.

[1] A Dutch florin is equal to about forty cents in United States currency.

4

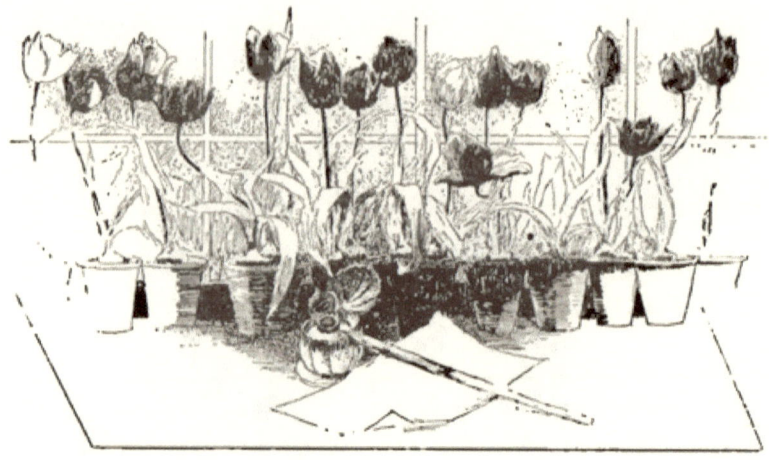

The owner of the first refused an offer for it of the fee simple of twelve acres of building lots. The second, that of Amsterdam, was finally sold for 4600 florins (1840 dollars), a new carriage, two gray horses, and a complete suit of harness! This statement is well attested, and is printed in the records of the day.

One Munsing, who wrote a large volume on the tulipomania, gives this list of articles which were delivered for a single root of the variety called *The Viceroy :*

"Two lasts [loads] of wheat; four lasts of rye; four fat oxen; eight fat swine; twelve fat sheep; two hogsheads of wine; four tuns of beer; one thousand pounds of cheese; a suit of clothes; a silver cup; a bed, complete, and two tuns of butter,— the whole valued at twenty-five hundred florins [or one thousand dollars]." And all for one root!

Still the mania grew. Men parted not only with their money, but with their lands, household goods, apparel, watches —anything, for the purchase of tulips.

People of all grades, from the rich burgomaster to the chimney-sweep, speculated in the flower. Ladies bought bulbs in the hope of making large profits upon them. The rise and fall in tulip stocks were the excitement of the day. At last, the government, becoming alarmed for the state of society, checked the traffic, and so burst the bubble. Then things were worse than ever. Disappointed and enraged speculators went to law; but the law turned its back upon them. It was decided that debts contracted under tulip-speculation were not legal. Then there *was* trouble!

But time, the great consoler quieted matters before very

A TULIP FANTASY.

long, and Holland settled down to its tobacco and meerschaum again. There had also been great tulip excitements in England and Paris, but these, too, died out in time.

To this day, however, the Hollanders are fond of their

turban-flower, as well they may be. A great tulip-bed, with its stately rows of gay flowers in their setting of soft, waving green, is a beautiful sight. But, to enjoy it to the utmost, one must love the flowers with true Dutch fondness and pride. Not only this, but he must dwell upon the special traits and charms of each specimen, as though it were a personal friend.

Verily, as I said at first, Holland is the queerest country that ever the sun shone upon! But the queerest thing of all is, when you really know much about it you feel more like crying than laughing; for this land that lies so loosely upon the sea has many a time been forced to be as a rock against a legion of foes. Its stanch-hearted people have suffered as never nation suffered before. Dutch country-folk look sleepy, I know, and have some very odd ways; but — Motley's history of the Rise of the Dutch Republic is not a funny book.

There is no more heartrending, terrible story in all history than that of the siege of Haarlem by the Spaniards in the sixteenth century. It cannot be told here; but one of its opening incidents shows the Spanish forces, unused to ice, tramping and tumbling toward Haarlem upon the frozen, slippery sea. Their object was to capture the Dutch ships that lay near the city, tightly held in by the ice. Suddenly they were overpowered. How? By a body of armed men on skates, who, springing from ice-trenches, flew swiftly upon the astonished Spaniards, shooting them down by hundreds. It was a day of victory for the Dutch patriots. But what months of terrible suffering, of almost superhuman endurance, came to them afterward!

CHARGE OF THE DUTCH SOLDIERS ON SKATES.

The ocean, too, could tell tales of Dutch sea-fights and Dutch ships bound on great enterprises; though it has a funny story of the brave admiral Van Tromp, which you may already have heard. He was born a little Dutchman, two hundred and ninety-seven years ago,—just two summers before the first tulip bowed upon Dutch soil. His father, who was an admiral, in due time took his little boy to sea. One day in a naval fight with the British, the father was killed, and little Marten Harpertzoon Van Tromp was taken prisoner. He was made to work as cabin-boy for many a weary month, but he did not despair. He was a Dutch boy.

In two years he was free again. Soon better fortunes came to him. In early manhood he entered the Dutch navy, and finally became Admiral of Holland, sometimes fighting against the Spaniards, sometimes beaten on the high seas, but oftener victorious. In fact, in the course of his career, he was winner of more than thirty battles. He had many a fierce sea-fight with Admiral Blake of England, and, though conquered by this enemy at last, he had the satisfaction of one victory over Blake so brilliant and thorough that he celebrated the event by sailing the British Channel with a broom fastened to his masthead. This was his way of proclaiming that he had swept his enemy from the seas.

CHAPTER VI

ND now let us see how Holland, from its earliest history, has proved itself to be truly a Land of Pluck:

In the old, old time, when many who now are called the' heroes of antiquity were cutting their baby-teeth, men began to quarrel for the possession of the country which is now known as Holland; and in one form or another, the contest has been going on nearly ever since. Why any should have coveted it, is a mystery to me. It was then only a low tract of spongy marsh, a network of queer rivers that seemed never to know where they belonged, but insisted every spring upon paying unwelcome visits to the inland—hiding here, running into each other there, and falling asleep in pleasant places. It was a great land-and-water kaleidoscope, girt about with a rim of gloomy forest; or a sort of dissected puzzle, with half of the pieces in soak; and its owners were a scanty, savage, fish-eating tribe, living like beavers on mounds of their own raising.

What could have tempted outsiders to disturb them? What, indeed, unless it were the same feeling that often makes a small boy holding either a kaleidoscope, or a puzzle, an object of persecution to all the big boys around him.

"Let *me* take a look!" they cry; "I want *my* turn"; or, "Give *me* the puzzle! Let's see what I can make out of it!"

You know how it is too apt to be. First, their attention is arrested by seeing the small boy peculiarly happy and absorbed. They begin to nudge, then to bully him. Small Boy shakes his head and tries to enjoy himself in peace and quietness. Bullying increases—the nudges become dangerous. In despair he soon gives in, or, rather, gives up, and the big boys slide into easy possession.

But suppose the small boy is plucky, and will not give up? Suppose he would see the puzzle crushed to atoms first? Suppose only positive big-boy power can overcome his as positive resistance? What then?

So began the history of Holland.

The first who held possession of Dutch soil—not the first who ever had lived upon it, but the first who had persistently enjoyed the kaleidoscope, and busied themselves with the puzzle—were a branch of the great German race. Driven by circumstances from their old home, they had settled upon an empty island in the river Rhine, which, you know, after leaving its pleasant southern country, straggles through Holland in a bewildered search for the sea. This island they called Betauw, or "Good Meadow," and so, in time, themselves came to be called Batavii, or Batavians.

Other portions of the country were held by various tribes living upon and beyond a great tract of land which afterward, in true Holland style, was turned into a sea,[1] called the Zuyder Zee. Most of these tribes were sturdy and brave, but the Batavii were braver than any. Fierce, stanch and defiant, they taught even their little children only the law of might; and their children grew up to be mightier than they. The blessed Teacher had not yet brought the world his lesson of mercy and love. "Conquer one another" had stronger claims to their consideration than "Love one another."

Their votes in council were given by the clashing of arms; and often their wives and mothers stood by with shouts and cries of encouragement wherever the fight was thickest. "Others go to battle," said the historian Tacitus; "these go to war."

Soon the all-conquering Romans, who, with Julius Cæsar at their head, had trampled surrounding nations into subjection, discovered that the sturdy Batavii were not to be vanquished—that their friendship was worth far more than the spongy country they inhabited. An alliance was formed, and the Batavii were declared to be exempt from the annual tax or tribute which all others were forced to pay to the Romans. Cæsar himself was not ashamed to extol their skill in arms, nor to send their

[1] The Zuyder Zee was formed by successive inundations during the thirteenth century. In the last of these inundations — in 1287 — nearly eighty thousand persons were drowned.

already famous warriors to fight his battles and strike terror to the hearts of his foes.

The Batavian cavalry could swim across wide and deep rivers without breaking their ranks, and their infantry were excelled by none in drill, in archery, and in wonderful powers of endurance. They had fought too long with the elements in holding their "Good Meadow" to be dismayed in battle by any amount of danger and fatigue.

The Romans called them "friends," but the Batavians soon discovered that they were being used merely as a cat's-paw. After a while, as cat's-paws will, they turned and scratched. A contest, stubborn and tedious, between the Romans and Batavians followed. At length both parties were glad to make terms of peace, which prevailed, with few interruptions, until the decline of the Roman Empire.

After that, hordes of barbarians overran Europe; and Holland, with the rest, had a hard time of it. Man to man, the Batavian could hold his own against any mortal foe, but he could not always be proof against numbers. The "Good Meadow," grown larger and more valuable, was conquered and held by several of the "big-boy" savage tribes, in turn, but not until Batavian pluck stood recorded in many a fearful tale passed from generation to generation.

Later, each of the surrounding nations, as it grew more powerful, tried to wrest Holland from the holders of her soil. Some succeeded for a time, some failed; but always, and every time, the Dutch gathered their strength for the contest and went not to battle, but to war. As, in later

BATAVIANS IN COUNCIL.—" DEATH TO THE INVADER!"

history, the Russians burned Moscow to prevent it from falling into the hands of Napoleon, so this stanch people always stood ready, at the worst, to drown Holland rather than yield her to the foe. Often they let in the waters they had laboriously shut out, laying waste hundreds of fertile acres, that an avenging sea might suddenly confound the invaders. Often they faced famine and pestilence,— men, women, and little wonder-stricken children perishing in the streets of their beleaguered cities—all who had breath to say it, still fiercely refusing to surrender. Wherever the strong arm of the enemy succeeded in mowing these people down, a stronger, sturdier growth was sure to spring from the stubble. Sometimes defeated, never subdued, they were patient under subjection only until they were again ready to rise as one man and throw off the yoke. Now and then, it is true, under promise of peace and increased prosperity, they formed a friendly union with a one-time enemy. But woe to the other side if it carried aggression and a trust in might too far. Treachery, oppression, breach of faith were sure, sooner or later, to arouse Dutch pluck; and Dutch pluck, in the end, has always beaten.

CHAPTER VII

THE DUTCH HAVE TAKEN HOLLAND

AND so, though Roman, Saxon, Austrian, Spaniard, Belgian, Englishman, and Frenchman in turn flourished a scepter over them, it comes, after all, to be true, that only "the Dutch have taken Holland." It is theirs by every right of inheritance and strife—theirs to hold, to drain, and to pump, for ever and ever. They wrested it from the sea, not in a day, but through long years of patient toil, through dreary years of suffering and sorrow. They have counted their dead, in their war with the ocean alone, by hundreds of thousands. Industry, hardihood, and thrift have been better allies to them than were Cæsar's Roman legions to the old Batavian forefathers.

For ages, it seems, Holland could not have known a leisure moment. Frugal, hardy, painstaking, and persevering, her spirit was ever equal to great enterprises. With her every difficulty was a challenge. Obstacles that would have discouraged others, inspired the Dutch with increased energy. Their land was only a marsh threatened by the sea. What of that? So much the more need of labor and skill to make it a hailing-place among nations. It was barren and bleak. " Why, then," said they, " so much the more need for us to become masters in tilling the soil." It was a very little place, scarcely worth a name on the maps. " So much the more need," said plucky Holland, " that we extend our possessions, gain lands in every corner of the earth, and send our ships far and near, until every nation shall unconsciously pay us tribute."

" Such is the industry of the people and the trade they drive," said a writer of the sixteenth century, " that, having little or no corn of their own growth, they do provide themselves elsewhere, not only sufficient for their own spending, but wherewith to supply their neighbors. Having no timber of their own, they spend more timber in building ships and fencing their water-courses than any country in the world. . . . And finally, having neither flax nor wool, they make more cloth of both sorts than is made in all the countries of the world, except France and England."

Of some things they soon began to have a surplus. There were not half nor a quarter enough persons in frugal Holland to drink all the milk of their herds. Forthwith Dutch butter and cheese came to be sent all over Christendom. The herring-fisheries were enormous. More fish came to their nets than would satisfy every man, woman, and child in Holland. England had enough herring of

5

"A FINE CATCH OF HERRING!"

her own. Ships were far too slow in those steamless days to make fresh fish a desirable article of export. Here was trouble! Not so. Up rose a Dutchman named William Beukles, to invent the curing and pickling of herring. The fish trade made Holland richer, more prosperous than ever. In time, a monument was raised to the memory of Beukles, for was he not a national benefactor?

The Dutch delight in honoring their heroes, their statesmen, and inventors. You cannot be long among them without hearing of one Laurens Janzoon Koster, to whom, they insist, the world owes the art of printing with movable types — the most important of human inventions. Their cities are rich in memorials and monuments of those whose wisdom and skill have proved a boon to mankind. All along the paths of human progress we can find Dutch footprints. In education, science, and political economy, they have, many a time, led the way.

The boys and girls of Holland are citizens in a high sense of the word. They soon learn to love their country, and to recognize the fatherly care of its government. The sense of common danger, and the necessity of all acting together in common defense, has served to knit the affections of the people. In truth it may be said, for history has proved it, that in every Dutch arm you can feel the pulse of Holland. Throughout her early struggles, in the palmy, glorious days of the republic, as well as now in her cautious constitutional monarchy, the Dutch have been patriots — mistaken and short-sighted at times, even goaded to cruel deeds by the brutal wickedness of their enemies, but always true to their beloved "Good Meadow."

Hollow-land, Low-land, or Netherland, whatever men may call it, their country stands high in their hearts. They love it with more than the love of a mountaineer for his native hills.

To be sure there have been riots and outbreaks there, as in all other thickly settled parts of the world—perhaps more than elsewhere, for Dutch indignation, though slow in kindling, makes a prodigious blaze when once fairly afire. Some of these disturbances have arisen only after a long endurance of serious wrongs; and some seem to have been started at once by that queer friction-match in human nature, which, if left unguarded, is sure to be nibbled at, and so ignited, by the first little mouse of discontent that finds it.

There was a curious origin to one of these domestic quarrels. On a certain occasion a banquet was given, at which were present two noted Dutch noblemen, rivals in power, who had several old grudges to settle. The conversation turning on the codfishery, one of the two remarked upon the manner in which the hook (*hoek*) took the codfish, or *kabbeljaauw*, as the Dutch call it.

"The hook take the codfish!" exclaimed the other in no very civil tone; "it would be better sense to say that the codfish takes the hook."

The grim jest was taken up in bitter earnest. High words passed, and the chieftains rose from the table enemies for life.

They proceeded to organize war against each other; a bitter war it proved to Holland, for it lasted one hundred and fifty years, and was fought out with all

THE ORIGIN OF THE CODFISH WAR. "THE GRIM JEST WAS TAKEN UP IN BITTER EARNEST."

5*

the stubbornness of family feuds. The opposing parties took the names of "hoeks" and "kabbeljaauws," and men of all classes enlisted in their respective ranks. In many instances fathers, brothers, sons, and old-time friends forgot their ties, and knew each other only as foes. The feud (being Dutch!) raged hotter and stronger in proportion as men had time coolly to consider the question. A thicket of mutual wrongs, real or imaginary, sprang up to further entangle the opposing parties; families were divided, miles of smiling country laid in ruin, and tens of thousands of men slain — for what?

Those who fought, and those who looked on, longing for peace, are alike silent now. Historical records do not quite clear up the mystery. We know how hard it must have been to settle the knotty question whether hooks or codfish can more properly be said to be " taken," and how dangerous the smallest thorns of anger and jealousy become if not plucked out promptly. It is certain, too, that the hoeks and kabbeljaauws were terribly in earnest, though what they killed each other for we "cannot well make out."

The kabbeljaauws had one advantage. When a public dinner was given by their party, the first dish brought in by the seneschal (or steward) was a huge plate of codfish elaborately decorated with flowers; something not ornamental only, but substantial and satisfactory; while the corresponding dish at a hoek festival contained nothing but a gigantic hook encircled by a flowery wreath.

All through Dutch history you will find quaint words and phrases that have a terrible record folded within their quaintness. The Casenbrotspel, or Bread and Cheese war, was not funny when it came to blight the last ten years of the fifteenth century, though its name sounds trivial now. And the Gueux, or " Beggars," who, nearly a century later, come forth on the bloodstained page, were something more than beggars, as King Philip and the wicked Duke of Alva found to their cost.

Ah, those Gueux! Watch for them when you read Dutch history. They will soon appear, with their wallets and wooden bowls, their doublets of ashen gray,— brave, reckless, desperate men, whose deeds struck terror over land and sea. When once they come in sight, turn as you may, you will meet them; you will hear their wild cry, "Long live the Beggars!" ringing amid the blaze and carnage of many a terrible day. There are princes and nobles among them. They will grow bolder and fiercer, more reckless and desperate, until their country's persecutor, Philip of Spain, has withdrawn the last man of all his butchering hosts from their soil; until the Duke of Alva, one of the blackest characters in all history, has cowered before the wrath of Holland!

Ah! my light-hearted boys and girls, if there were not lessons to be learned from these things, it would be well to blot them from human memory. But would it be well to forget the heroism, the majestic patience, the trust in God, that shine forth resplendent from these darkest pages of Dutch history? Can we afford to lose such examples of human grandeur under suffering as come to us from the beleaguered cities of Naarden, Haarlem, and Leyden? When you learn their stories, if you do not know them

THE GUEUX, OR BEGGARS.

already, you will understand Dutch pluck in all its full-
ness, and be glad that, in the end, it proved victorious
over every foe.

But, as you have been told before, it is not only amid
the din of war that Holland has shown her pluck; nor is
hers the bragging, boisterous quality that offends at every
turn. A simpler, firmer, more peacefully inclined people
it would be hard to find; but somehow they have an odd
way of being actively concerned in the history of other
nations. Possibly this is due to the fact that their peculiar simplicity and love of quiet have proved a sort of
standing invitation to those who would make war with
them; possibly it is because of their great commercial
enterprise, and their tempting stores; but, to my mind,
their remarkably far-seeing, though seemingly sleepy, way
of looking at things, has had much to do with their
progress. They seem never to threaten, yet always to
perform; never to prepare, but always to be ready.

THE COFFEE-HOUSE.

CHAPTER VIII

THE DUTCH AT HOME AND ABROAD

THE story of Dutch patriotism could be written out in symbols, or pictures, more eloquently than that of any other nation. There would be shields, arrows and spears, and battleships and fortresses, and all the paraphernalia of war, ancient and modern. But beside these, and having a sterner significance, would be the tools and implements of artisans; the windmills, the dikes, the canals; the sluice-gates, the locks; the piles that hold up their cities. How much could be told by the great, white-sailed merchantmen bound for every sea; by the mammoth docks, and by the wonderful cargoes coming and going! How the great buildings would loom up, each telling its story—the factories, warehouses, schools, colleges, museums, legislative halls, the hospitals, asylums, and churches!

There would be more than these: there would be libra-
ries, art-galleries, and holy places battered and broken.
There would be monuments and relics, and church organs
—chief among them that of the Haarlem Cathedral, to

THE HAARLEM CATHEDRAL.

this day ranking among the grandest in the world. There
would be boats manned by rough heroes trying to save
thousands of drowning fellow-creatures whose homes had
been swept away by the waves. We should see 'some of
the most beautiful public parks of their time; gardens, too,

wonderful in their blooming ; and, over all, the bells — the
faithful carillons that for ages have sent down messages,
more or less musical, upon the people.

DUTCH pluck has accomplished, and will yet accomplish,
wonders. Even now, while the waves of the great Zuyder
Zee are beating against its dikes, Holland is deciding
whether a vast portion of this sea shall be changed back
to what it was in the thirteenth century — dry land!
A tremendous piece of work, indeed ; but it will be done if
the Dutchmen say so. Here is the small bit of very big
news as it came to the "London Times" from the capital
of Holland, in this year of grace, 1894:

"The Hague, May 5.—The Royal Commission, presided
over by M. Lely, Minister of the Waterstaat, which has
long been studying the scheme for the draining and reclaim-
ing of the Zuyder Zee, has concluded its labors. Twenty-
one members out of the twenty-six composing the Commission recommend that the projected work be carried out
by the State.

"It is proposed to reclaim from the sea about 450,000
acres, the value of which is estimated at 326,000,000 guilders.[1] The cost of this important work is computed at
189,000,000 guilders, or with the accumulated expenditure,
including measures of defense and the payment of com-
pensation to the fishermen of the Zee, at 315,000,000 guilders. The draining is to be carried out by means of a sea
dike from northern Holland into Friesland."

[1] $130,400,000, as the guilder — like the silver florin — is equal to
forty cents of United States money.

Dutch pluck has sailed all over the world. It has put its stamp on commerce, science, and manufactures. It has set its seal on every quarter of the earth. Dutchmen were at home in Japan before either the Americans or English had dared to intrude upon those inhospitable shores. There were great obstacles to encounter in any attempt at trading or becoming acquainted with that strange hermit of an empire in the east. She had enough of her own, she said, and asked no favors of the outside barbarians. Would they be kind enough to stay away? Most of the world gave an unwilling assent; but Holland undertook to show Japan the folly of rejecting the benefits of commerce; and in time, and after many a hard struggle, succeeded in establishing a Japanese trade.

Talking of ships, whence did the ship sail that brought the good Fathers of New England safely across the sea? And, for months before, what country had sheltered them from the persecution that threatened them in their native land? Ask the books these questions, if need be, and ask yourselves whether to shelter the oppressed, to offer an asylum to innocent but hunted fugitives from every clime, is not a noble work for pluck to do.

Whence, too, did some of our New York oddities come? Why are you, little New Yorkers, so fond of waffles, crullers, doughnuts, and New Year's cake? Dutch inventions every one of them. Why do you expectantly honor the good St. Nicholas, the patron saint of New York? Why is this city turned topsyturvy in a general "moving" whenever the first of May comes round? Why, until very recently, did your fathers and uncles on the first day of

January, from morning till night, pay visits from house to house, wishing the ladies a " Happy New Year " ?   Simply because these were Holland customs. The Americans of the day only were following the example long ago set them by the Dutch.

Hendrik Hudson, the first white man who explored our noble North River, was an adopted Dutchman.   He modestly called it De Groote (or the Great) River, little thinking that for all time after it would be known as the Hudson.   Staten (or States) Island was so named by him in honor of his home government, the States-General.

At that time he was in the service of the Dutch East India Company.   Three years later he made another voyage and discovered the famous bay, far to our northward, which now bears his name.   Intrepid as he was, the bitter cold of that region, and threatened starvation, prevented him from carrying out his resolve to spend the winter on the shores of his bay, and he set sail for home, only to meet the tragic fate which to this day is veiled in mystery. The sailors mutinied, and set him afloat, with eight other men, in an open boat.   They were never seen nor heard of again.

It is said that Hudson gave the name Helle Gat, or Beautiful Pass, to the dangerous waterway between Long Island and Manhattan Island which in 1885, only nine years ago, yielded its most dangerous reef, Flood Rock, to the persuasions of science and dynamite.

The site of the present capital of the State of New York at first was called New Orange, in honor of William, Prince of Orange and Stadtholder of Holland; but in 1664,

A FIRESIDE IN OLD NEW YORK.

6

when the English were in power, they changed the name to Albany, after the Duke of York and Albany, better known to you, perhaps, by his later title, King James II. of England.

Look at the names of many down-town streets of New York city, once called New Amsterdam,—Cortlandt, Vandam, Roosevelt, Stuyvesant, and scores of others all named after good Dutchmen. Not only New York, but Brooklyn, Albany, and other cities have streets that lead one directly into the Netherlands, so to speak. Indeed, Dutch names lie sprinkled very thickly within a hundred miles of Fifth Avenue in every direction. You readily may suspect the origin of Harlem, named when it was a little hamlet quite far from New Amsterdam, but connected with it by a country road known as the Bouerie. This Bouerie, or Bowerie, now spelled Bowery, no longer has the rural, bower-like aspect it enjoyed in those old days; for then it was a road through the farm or *bouerie* of Peter Stuyvesant, the last Dutch colonial governor of these New Netherlands.

Few New-Yorkers nowadays stop to ask why Eleventh street, which extends across the city from the East to the North River, should break off at Fourth Avenue and begin again on the west side of Broadway. But they know that a long solid block—its southwestern corner beautified by Grace Church and its parsonage—reaches from Tenth street to Twelfth street. The fact is, Eleventh street was stopped just there by a Dutchman, or an honored citizen of Dutch descent, named Brevoort. Mrs. Lamb, in her "History of New York," tells us that the mansion of Henry

Brevoort fronted the Bowery road, and, according to the plans of the street commissioners, Eleventh street would cut across the site occupied by his house. He resisted the opening of the street with such determination and effect " that the block remained undisturbed. To this day, Eleventh street has no passageway between Broadway and Fourth Avenue."

And in Grace Church, near the south entrance, may be seen a memorial tablet of white marble, the leading inscription of which reads :

IN MEMORY OF

HENRY BREVOORT

WHO DIED AUG. 21. 1841 IN THE 94. YEAR OF HIS AGE IN POSSESSION OF THE GROUND ON WHICH THIS CHURCH NOW STANDS ; DERIVED IN UNBROKEN DESCENT FROM THE FIRST COLONISTS OF NEW NETHERLANDS.

HOLLAND is stanch, true, and plucky, but it *is* Holland; and, lest you forget that it still is the oddest country in Christendom, I must tell you that within a few years a new king has succeeded to its throne—and this new king is a bright little girl not yet fifteen years of age! Yes, the High Council of Holland solemnly decreed that officials and other public servants should take the oath of allegiance, not to Queen but to *King* Wilhelmina! The Dutch newspapers protested vehemently against this form, as being contrary to common sense. But the High Court of Holland does not yield to dictation, and the press, it seems, at last adopted a dignified silence in the matter. Possibly the expression "King Wilhelmina" may recall to some readers that historic incident of 1740, when the heroic young Empress of Austria, beset with foes, heard her impassioned Hungarian nobles shouting, as their swords leaped from their scabbards: "Let us die for our King, Maria Theresa!"

6*

But, king or queen, this royal little Wilhelmina of Holland already rules in the hearts of her people. Well may the boys and girls of our republic follow her career with interest;—so bright, winning, and unaffected is she in her pretty dignity and her earnest patriotic spirit. Despite her high station, she is a real child, ready for play and, as a recent writer tells us, "devotedly fond of dolls."

On one occasion, it is said, her youthful majesty was heard addressing a refractory doll as follows: "Now be good and quiet, because if you don't I will turn you into a queen, and then you will not have any one to play with at all."

Poor little doll-mother! In the confidence of *that* family circle she may say things that she hardly could utter at court receptions! To some of her dolls, however, she undoubtedly shows a dignified reserve ; for instance, to the fifty lately given to her on her fourteenth birthday by her mother, the queen regent. They are stiff and imposing, we may be sure, for they are dressed to represent soldiers of rank, in order that the little queen may become familiar with, and easily recognize, the different uniforms of the officers in her Dutch army.

———

In concluding these simple chapters about the Land of Pluck, I yield to an impulse to quote—for the benefit of readers who would like a further familiar word about the Holland of to-day—some extracts from two personal letters recently received. The first is from an American

QUEEN WILHELMINA OF HOLLAND, AT THE AGE OF ELEVEN.
(FROM A PHOTOGRAPH BY KAMEKE, THE HAGUE, NETHERLANDS.)

friend traveling through the Netherlands. The other was written by a young girl born and bred in Holland.

"THE HAGUE, March 28, 189-.

" . . . Heaven bless the Dutchmen! They are the most delightful and sterling folk that we have found in all Europe! And no more charming days have we had anywhere than at Amsterdam, at Haarlem, and at The Hague and Scheveningen. . . . At Amsterdam we saw the Great Dike and the lesser dikes (worthy monuments to the sturdy force of this brave race), and at Zaandam, near by, we went through a perfect forest of windmills, of which there are nearly four hundred within the town limits. A more picturesque sight cannot be imagined. As the little steamboat got into the thick of them, with those huge arms whirling close by on every side, the whole landscape began to take on the motion, and I half expected the boat would turn a somersault any moment. But it was a fascinating spectacle.

" . . . And the little cottages alongside the stream— how quaint and cozy! And every street in Amsterdam, and every woman and child — how clean and fair and tidy they look! And the delightful head-gear that the country women wear! And the happy, healthy smiles of the boys and girls! The virtues of these honest Dutch folk shine out to eyes that have just seen the Italian paupers. Small as it is, Holland can take care of itself. For a thousand years the Dutch have fought the sea, and for eighty years they fought the greatest military power of Europe, and always held their own.

"In all our travels we have found no race so sturdy and independent as this, so healthy and seemingly so happy. Not a beggar have we seen in Holland, but we *have* seen the origin of many of the best characteristics of New York life. I never realized till now how much our big city owes to the Dutchmen. . . . And these people are not only the tidiest folk in the world, and among the bravest, cheeriest, and most upright, but they also have an inborn, genuine love of art. It is a significant fact that the only place in Europe in which we have seen the people of the country actually enjoying their great pictures, was in the Ryks Museum at Amsterdam. The great building was crowded with Dutch folk of all classes, and of a hundred different types — all really interested in the pictures. It was a study to watch them.

"And the pictures themselves! The Dutchmen of to-day may well appreciate them. You remember Rembrandt's famous 'Night Watch' and his portrait of an old woman, at Amsterdam, and his celebrated 'Anatomist,' here at The Hague. I have seen now many of the most famous paintings in the world, but for perfection of technical skill these of Rembrandt's surely are equal to the best. True, he did not paint ideal subjects, nor enter the spiritual realm — in which the Italian masters were so great. But as a portrait-painter he seems to me the greatest of all the masters.

". . . But I must restrain my enthusiasm, and tell you briefly that we have 'done' also the Amsterdam 'Zoo' (one of the finest zoölogical gardens in the world), have heard the great organ of Haarlem, have seen two rich private galleries, have heard the 'Mikado' sung in Dutch (fairly well sung, too, but with some nightmare words fitted to the music), have seen 'Peter the Great's hut' at Zaandam,—and to-day an auction of fish on the beach at Scheveningen, with the fishermen and white-capped fisherwomen thronging about in their odd costumes and big wooden shoes. . . . To-morrow we return to Amsterdam."

Holland speaks for itself, and every traveler is its interpreter. But here is an inside, home letter straight from the land of dikes. Its writer, a bright and patriotic Dutch girl, is in herself the best evidence one can have of the advantages of education her country offers to all.

It cannot but be encouraging to young Americans trying to master a foreign language to note how admirably this young Hollander expresses herself in English. Not a word of her clearly written letter has been changed:

" SCHEVENINGEN, Feb. 28, 189–.

" . . . The winter has been, as probably everywhere else, exceptionally cold; an old-fashioned winter, and one that will be recorded in the annals of history and not soon forgotten. Of course, it has been the cause of much poverty and misery, and every one was thankful when, after weeks of severe frost, the thaw fell in; but much has been done to soften the sufferings of the poor, and those who went round to ask for help did not ask in vain. On the other hand, the whole country was alive with wholesome merriment, caused by the skating that was practised over the whole length and width of our watery little land.

Holland is very characteristic and very much at its advantage during such a time, and I am really thankful to have been able to join in the universal movement.

"As you know, a great many of the people, especially the peasants, skate very well. The country is cut up by canals running from one town to the other, and from one village to the other; along these waters slow barges travel peacefully the whole summer through, laden with coals, wood, vegetables, pottery, and numberless other things; a great deal of traffic is done in this slow but sure way, as it is a very cheap mode of transport. But these same waters now bore a much livelier aspect. People of all classes skated along their smooth surfaces, and many have been the expeditions planned and executed to skate from one town to the other, halting at several small villages on the way, and thus seeing the country in an original and very pleasant manner. . . .

"My sister and I, and several ladies and gentlemen, made a charming excursion on one of the finest and mildest days of the winter. The sun shone brightly, the sky was blue, and although the thermometer pointed below zero, it was quite warm and delicious to skate. We were quite a large party, and went from the Hague to Amsterdam, and thence across the Y and farther over the inland waters to Monnickendam, on skates of course.

"Monnickendam lies at the Zuider Zee, which is a kind of bay formed by the North Sea and surrounded by several provinces of our country. In comparison with your grand lakes, it is small, but we consider it quite a large water, and it is very rarely frozen over. This year, how-

IN SUMMER-TIME — ON THE CANAL.

ever, it was one immense surface of ice, stretching itself out as far as the eye could reach. It was quite *the* thing this winter to go out and see it; so, of course, we went there and visited the small island of Marken, which is situated near the coast.

". . . A small steamer goes daily from Monnickendam to the island, or three times a week—I 'm not sure about that; now all the communication was done by sledge and on skates over the ice. Thousands of people have seen Marken this winter in that way, and the place is quite a curiosity, especially for strangers. (If you happen to have a map of the Netherlands you 'll be sure to find where it lies in the Zuider Zee.)

"The quaint costumes worn by the peasant men and women are alone well worth the voyage to the place, being quite different from those worn in Scheveningen, and besides the pokey little wooden houses are charming in their way, and exceedingly clean and neat, with rows of colored earthenware dishes along the walls, and carved chests and painted wooden boxes piled one on the top of the other containing their clothes. Although so near the civilized world these good people live quite apart, hardly ever marry some one not from the island, and seem quite contented. They earn their living by fishing, and occasionally get as far as a harbor of Scotland.

"When we arrived at Marken across the ice we were very hungry, and on asking a peasant if he could procure us something to eat, were very hospitably received in his little house by his wife, who regaled us on bread, cheese, and milk. Enormous hunches of bread! but what will a

A WOMAN OF ZEELAND.

hungry skater not eat ?   And we sat very snugly in their
little room, admiring all their funny little contrivances.

   " . . . The Zuider Zee was very curious and interesting
to see.   Fancy an enormous field of ice crowded with thousands of people all on skates, and, moving swiftly between
them, brightly painted sledges with strong horses and jing-

ling bells, looking very picturesque. Also little ice-boats with large sails that come flying across the frozen waters, looking like great birds, but keeping at a little distance from the crowd for fear of accidents. A fair was held on the ice, where were going on all kinds of harmless amusements; and there were tents where they sold cakes and steaming hot milk and chocolate. The whole scene, the bright, moving, joyous crowd, made me think of the pictures by the old masters, like Teniers and Ostade, it was so thoroughly Dutch. But to think that this immense solid surface, whereon you moved so confidently, would melt again before the year was much older and change itself into lapping waves! It was hardly conceivable! . . .

" At the Hague we have a very prettily situated skating-club, where our little circle of friends saw each other daily and where we spent many a pleasant hour. So the winter has flown by. It is not quite over, but it seems so to me, as the last weeks have been very fine, and the place where we live, being half country, directly takes a spring-like air. Tennis begins to reign supreme, and I am going to practise this game very seriously.

" . . . I have not heard much music this winter. Our German opera, which grew poorer and poorer every year, is now gone altogether, and that was the only way in which we heard some Wagnerian operas, which I like above all others; indeed, the more you hear them the less you care about the others. Once a fortnight I regularly go to the concert, but there are times when I can't listen to the music. My mind strays, and try as much as I will, the sounds pass over me and don't leave any impression; I think the reason

7

of this is that I have heard too much music in the last few years, and that I don't appreciate it. So when it is not something I like very much I had rather not hear it, as I think it only needlessly fatigues my brain, and so I do not profit by it at all. . . .

" Your letter was very pleasant and so fluently written! I wish I could do as well. My only consolation is that it is not my language; but then I cannot produce such a good style in Dutch either, and you will hardly believe it, but I need a dictionary more when I write a Dutch letter than when I write an English one. Of course I make a great many mistakes in English, but Dutch is a far more difficult language, and you never know when a word is masculine or feminine (unless you are exceedingly clever!), as it makes no difference when you speak, but a great difference when you write; so if you want to write correctly you *have* to look in the dictionary or else to guess. Then you say, 'Oh! that word is probably feminine,' and you change the sentence accordingly, and afterward you discover that you were quite wrong. Is not that a troublesome language ? The French can hear when to put ' le ' or ' la ' before the word (at least they rarely make mistakes), but we can't. It sounds all the same when speaking.

" . . . The year that has gone has been very much like the foregoing ones except for some political events which have created a change in our country. Our old king died, as you remember, and at his death there was a sincere mourning over the whole country. Personally he was not so very much liked; still his subjects were attached to him because he was (his two sons having died) the last

A STREET IN THE HAGUE.

male descendant of a glorious and highly respected race: the House of Orange. The Oranges are loved by the Dutch because they can boast of many a valorous and wise ancestor, but principally because the head of the house, Prince William, who was murdered in 1584, freed the people from the Spanish tyrant whose despotic reign had become unbearable.

"The sole descendant of this long list of princes and kings is our little Queen Wilhelmina, much beloved by the people, who cherish her as something very precious. The government is now in the hands of her mother, who is queen regent until the little one is eighteen years old. Queen Emma is a very superior woman, kind and wise, giving her little daughter a sensible education, and quite capable of filling her difficult position and of executing her duties exceedingly well.

"Of course you, like a true American, do not feel any enthusiasm for kings and queens, but our government is constitutional and liberal, and I don't think the people have in reality much more freedom in any of the new republics than in our kingdom. The two queens live in the Hague. As yet, of course, everything is very quiet at the court, but the mother and daughter can be seen daily when driving out, looking very happy together. They pass our house nearly every day. I would not be a queen for anything — would you? Fancy not a bit of freedom, not being able to move a step without the whole land, so to say, knowing of it; their sorrows and rejoicings public sorrows and rejoicings! Seemingly rulers of the land, but in reality dictated to in their slightest acts!

7*

"As yet all goes well in our little country, and I don't think we need have any fear of being swallowed up by the great states that surround us.

". . . And now, my dear L., it is really time to finish this long letter. I think I never wrote such a long one before. . . .   ELSIE M—."

"ALL goes well in our little country." Cheery words, these, from a daughter of the race.

Long may all go well with sturdy, steadfast Holland, girt with grim dikes higher than the tallest of its foes; the land of whirling sails and leaning seas; the great little land of oddity, thrift, patriotism—and pluck!

DAY-DREAMS ON THE DIKE

"FIVE STOUT LITTLE HOLLANDERS, ALL SITTING IN THE BROAD, BRIGHT SUNLIGHT — DREAMING!"

DAY-DREAMS ON THE DIKE

THERE were five of them,— Dirk van Dorf, Katrina van Dorf, Greitje Kuyp, Kassy Riker, and Ludoff Kleef,— five stout little Hollanders, all well and happy, and all sitting in the broad, bright sunlight—dreaming!

It was not so at first, you must know. They had been trudging along the great dike,— their loose wooden shoes beating the hard clay—laughing a little, talking less, yet with an air of goodfellowship about them — these chubby little neighbor children, who knew one another so well that by a nod or a gesture, or by throwing a quick glance or a smile, they could take one another's meaning and make two words do the work of twenty. Their fathers and mothers were thrifty, hard-working folk living in Volendam, a little fishing-village hard by, built under one of the dikes of the Zuyder Zee.

The children, being Hollanders, knew quite well that the dike they were treading was a massive, wide bank or

wall built to keep back the sea that was forever trying to
spread itself over Holland, though Holland by no means
intended to allow it to do any such thing. And they
knew also, as did all Volendam, that Jan van Riper had
been out over long in his little fishing-boat, and that there had

been heavy winds
after he started;
also that his wife,
who was continually
scolding him, was
now going about,
her eyes red with
weeping, telling the
neighbors how good
and easy he was,
and how he would
n't harm a kitten
—Jan would n't!
They knew, more-
over, that Adrian
Runckel's tulip-bed
was a show; hardly
another man in the
village had a flower worth looking at, if you went in for
size, color, and stiffness. They knew, besides, that ever
so many queer flapping and squirming things had been
hauled in that very morning by Peter Loop's big net—
only he was dreadfully cross, and would n't let a body
come near it—that is, a little body. Above all, they
knew that the mother of Ludoff Kleef was coming to join

"HE WOULD N'T HARM A KITTEN—JAN WOULD N'T."

them as soon as she could finish up her dairy-work, and make herself and the children tidy. All the party need do was to keep along the dike and be good, and take care of little Ludolf, and sit down and rest whenever they felt like resting, and of all things they were not to soil or tear their clothes. So you see they were neither empty-headed nor careworn, nor were they in any danger of falling asleep; yet there they sat, on the dike, side by side, dreaming!

Kassy Riker was the first to glide into a dream, though sitting close beside little Ludolf, who wriggled, and wondered why his mother and sister and baby brother did n't come. He wanted to cry, but he felt in the depth of his baby soul that Kassy would laugh at him if he did; and as for the others, Greitje Kuyp was gazing a hundred miles out to sea already; Katrina van Dorf was so busy with her knitting that she had forgotten there was such a thing as a small boy in the world; and big boy Dirk van Dorf—why, he was altogether too grand a person to be moved by any amount of howling. So poor little Ludolf amused himself by watching a long straw that in the still air hitched itself along till it wavered feebly on the edge of the dike, uncertain whether to stay on shore or start on a seafaring career. If the straw had settled upon any definite course of action, Ludolf would have done the same; but, as it was, Ludolf kept on watching and watching it until, in the stillness, he forgot all about being a little boy who wanted his mother; for was not the straw whisking one end feebly, and turning round to begin again?

Meantime Greitje Kuyp gazed out to sea, the great

Zuyder Zee, wondering why any one should think it was
trying to come ashore and do mischief. It was so quiet,
so grand, and it bore the big fishing-smacks so patiently,
when it could so easily topple them over! Mother was
patient and peaceful, too. Greitje herself (so went her
day-dream) would be just like Mother, one of these days:
she would sew and mend and churn and bake, only she
would make more cakes and less bread. Yes, she would
bake great chests full of cinnamon-cakes,—*kaneel koekjes*,—
such as they sold at the Kermis; and she would be, oh,
just as good and kind to *her* little girl as Mother was to
her, and—

*   *   *

"I'm not going to stay at home all my life," Kassy
Riker was thinking or dreaming. "Some day I shall
keep a beautiful shop in Amsterdam, and sell laces and
caps and head-gear and lovely things; and I'll courtesy
and say '*ja, mijnheer*,' like a grand lady; and I'll learn
to sing and dance better than any girl at the Kermis;
and I shall wear gold on my temples, and have a lovely
jacket for skating-days; and every month I'll come back
for a while, and bring pretty things to Father, Mother, and
the minister; and—"

*   *   *

"I've done full a finger-length of it to-day," mused
Katrina, as she pressed her red lips together and worked
steadily at the chain she was weaving on a pin-rack
for her father. "It shall be done by his birthday, and
I'll hang his big silver watch on it while he's asleep,
and then kiss and hug him till he opens his eyes. Ah,

how we all will wish him a happy day and the Lord's
blessing ! And if he gives me a little cart some time for
my dog 'Shag' to draw, I think I 'll fill it full of wet,
shining fish and sell them at the market-town. No; I 'll
help Mother very hard at making the cheeses; and I 'll
fill the cart with them ; and soon Mother can have a fine
new lace cap with the money, and a silk apron; and maybe
I 'll be so useful to the family that they 'll decide to take
me out of school; and then—and then I 'll work and I 'll
save, and save, till perhaps—"

*   *   *

"Can *that* be Jan van Riper's boat ?" mused big boy
Dirk, as he eyed a fishing-smack just coming into view.
"No, it 's my uncle Ryk's. Like enough, Jan has landed
somewhere and put off to foreign parts, as he often says
he will when Vrouw van Riper's tongue gets too lively.
I should. I 'd like to go to foreign parts, anyway. Lots
of room for a fellow in Java; lots of rich Hollanders there
—we Hollanders own it, they say; and there 's no reason
a fellow like me should n't grow to be a merchant and
own warehouses, and—"

*   *   *

So the dreams ran on,— Greitje's, Kassy Riker's,
Katrina's, and Dirk van Dorf's,—all different, and all very
absorbing. Meantime the straw had shown itself so weak-
minded and tedious that little Ludoff had nodded himself
into a doze as he leaned against Greitje's plump little
shoulder. The dreaming time, pleasant as it was, had
really not been very long ; for even a smooth sea, a soft
summer breeze, and five serene little Dutch natures could

not have kept ten young legs and ten young arms quiet any longer.

A great shout from the village came faintly to the children's ears. Jan's boat was in sight! The little folk were up and alert in an instant. They turned about, to look back toward the village,—and if there was not Ludoff's mother, Mevrouw [1] Kleef, erect and smiling, coming briskly along the dike toward them! How handsome she looked, with her bright eyes and rosy cheeks, and the big lace cap, the blue-and-black short skirt, and the low jacket over the gaily-colored underwaist! Her little Troide toddled beside her, taking two steps to the mother's one, with deep blue eyes fixed upon the line of familiar forms just risen from the dike. The baby—it was a boy; one could tell *that* by the woolen *slaapmuts*, or nightcap, on his head, for the girl-babies in Volendam never wear that kind—the baby, trig and smart, gazed from the mother's arms at the same five familiar little forms, and in a moment the children all were crowding around the mevrouw.

"Jan is back, is n't he?" asked Dirk.

"Yes, I suppose so," she answered carelessly. The good woman was rather tired of her neighbor Jan van Riper's frequent misbehavings and false alarms.

"My, how warm the day!" she added, gently setting the baby down upon the turf beside her; "and the dear child is as weighty as a keg of herring!"

"Oh, oh, the beauty!" exclaimed the girls, quite enraptured with the little one; while Dirk and Ludoff

[1] *Mevrouw*, Madam (pronounced Meffrouw).

"LUDOFF'S MOTHER, MEVROUW KLEEF, WAS COMING BRISKLY ALONG THE DIKE."

doubled their fists, and pretended (to his great delight) they were going to pummel him soundly.

"Yes," said the mother. "He's a bouncing little man, and with a good head of his own. I was saying to myself as I came along that I should n't wonder if he should get to be a grand burgomeister some day, and rule a city, and lift us all to greatness—and so you shall, my little one! There, there, don't pull my skirt off, my Ludoff!" Then, looking brightly from one to another of the group, Mevrouw Kleef asked:

"And what have you been doing—you, Dirk, Katrina, and the rest of you?"

"Nothing," answered the children; but they all looked very happy. Day-dreams linger about us, you know, and light our way even when they are half forgotten.

"And now, my children," she continued, "we are to have a great pleasure, for I shall take you all to see the men start Raff Ootealt's new windmill this very afternoon. Raff is to make a short speech, and there will be music and dancing and a little feast."

"Good, good!" cried the happy little crowd, eager to set off at once.

So the mother took up her little burgomeister, and, rosy and smiling, started on her way back to the village, the children trudging after.

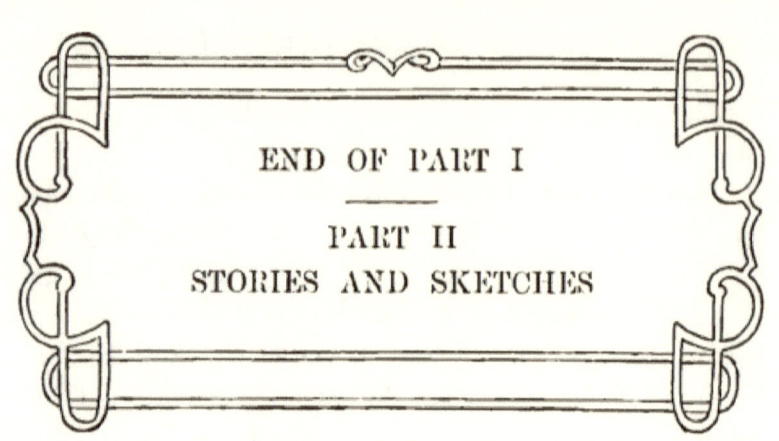

END OF PART I

PART II
STORIES AND SKETCHES

WONDERING TOM

"OH, TOM! THE KING WISHES TO SPEAK WITH YOU!"

Long, long ago, in a great city whose name is forgotten, situated on a river that ran dry in the days of Cinderella, there lived a certain boy, the only son of a poor widow. He had such a fine form and pleasant face that one day, as he loitered on his mother's door-step, the King stopped on the street to look at him.

"Who is that boy?" asked his Majesty of his Prime Minister.

This question brought the entire royal procession to a standstill.

The Prime Minister did not know, so he asked the Lord of the Exchequer. The Lord of the Exchequer asked the High Chamberlain; the High Chamberlain asked the Master of the Horse; the Master of the Horse asked the Court Physician; the Court Physician asked the Royal Rat-Catcher; the Royal Rat-Catcher asked the Chief-Cook-and-Bottle-Washer; and the Chief-Cook-and-Bottle-Washer asked a little girl named Wisk.

Little Wisk, with a pretty courtesy, informed him that the boy's name was Wondering Tom.

8*   117

"So, ho!" said the Chief-Cook-and-Bottle-Washer, telling the Royal Rat-Catcher. "So, ho!" said the Royal Rat-Catcher, passing on the news; and it traveled in that way until, finally, the Prime Minister, bowing low to the King, said:

"May it please your most tremendous Majesty, it's Wondering Tom."

"Tell him to come here!" said the King to the Prime Minister. "His Majesty commands him to come here!" was repeated to the next in rank; and again his words traveled through the Lord of the Exchequer, the High Chamberlain, the Master of the Horse, the Court Physician, the Royal Rat-Catcher, and the Chief-Cook-and-Bottle-Washer, until they reached little Wisk, who called out:

"Oh, Tom! the King wishes to speak with you."

"With me!" exclaimed Tom, never budging. "Why?"

"I don't know," returned little Wisk, "but you must go at once."

"*Why?*" cried Tom.

"Oh, Tom! Tom! they're going to kill you," she cried, in an agony.

"WHY? What for?" shouted Tom, staring in the wildest astonishment.

Surely enough, the Master of Ceremonies had ordered forth an executioner with a bowstring. In that city, any man, woman, or child who disregarded the King's slightest wish was instantly put to death.

The man approached Tom. Another second, and the bowstring would have done its work; but the King held up his royal hand in token of pardon, and beckoned Tom to draw near.

"Whatever in all this world can his Majesty want with me?" pondered the bewildered boy, moving very slowly toward the monarch.

"Well, sir!" said his Majesty, scowling. "So you are here at last! Why do they call you Wondering Tom?"

"ME, your Majesty?" faltered Tom. "I—I—don't know."

"You don't know? (Most remarkable boy, this!) And what were you doing, sir, when we sent for you?"

"Nothing, your Majesty. I was only wondering whether—"

"Ah, I see. You take your life out in wondering. A fine, strong fellow like you has no right to be idling in his mother's doorway. A pretty kingdom we should have if all our subjects were like this! You may go.

"He has a good face," continued the King, turning to the Prime Minister, "but he 'll never amount to anything."

"Ah, exactly so," said the Prime Minister. "Exactly so," echoed the Lord of the Exchequer, and "Exactly so," sighed the Chief-Cook-and-Bottle-Washer at last, as the royal procession passed on.

Tom heard it all.

"Now, how do they know that?" he muttered, scratching his head as he lounged back to the door-step. "Why in the world do they think I 'll never amount to anything?"

In the doorway he fell to thinking of little Wisk.

"What a very nice girl she is! I wonder if she 'd play with me if I asked her,—but I can't ask her. I do wonder what makes me so afraid to talk to Wisk!"

Meantime, little Wisk, who lived in the next house, watched him shyly.

"Tom!" she called out at last, swaying herself lithely round and round her wooden door-post, "the blackberries are ripe."

"You don't say so!" exclaimed Tom, in surprise.

"Yes, I do. And, Tom, there are bushels of them in the woods just outside of the city gates."

"Oh!" answered Tom, "I wonder if there are!"

"I *know* it," said little Wisk, decidedly, "and I 'm going to get some."

"Dear me!" thought Tom, "I wonder if she 'd like to have me go with her. Wisk!"

"What, Tom?"

"Oh, nothing," said the frightened fellow, suddenly changing his mind, "I was only wondering whether it is going to rain or not."

"Rain? Of course not," laughed little Wisk, as she ran off to join a group of children going toward the north city-gate; "but even if it should rain, what matter?"

"Oh," thought Tom, "she 's really gone for blackberries! I wondered what she had that little kettle on her arm for. Pshaw! Why did n't I tell her that I 'd like to go too?"

Just then his mother came to the door, clapping a wet ruffle between her hands. She was a clear-starcher.

"Tom, Tom! why *don't* you set about something! There 's plenty to do, in doors and out, if you 'd only think so."

"Yes, ma'am," said Tom, wondering whether or not he was going to have a scolding.

"But you look pale, my pet; go and play. Do. One does n't often have such a perfect day as this (and such

splendid drying, too!). If I were you, I'd make the
most of it"; and the mother went back into the bare
entry, still clapping the ruffle.

"I do wonder how I can make the most of it," asked
Tom of himself, over and over again, as he sauntered off.

He did n't dare to go toward the north gate of the city,
because he could n't decide what he should say if he
should meet little Wisk; so he turned toward the south.

"Shall I go back, I wonder, or keep on?" thought Tom,
as he found himself going farther from the door-step and
nearer to the great city-wall, until at last the southern
gate was reached. Following the dusty highway leading
from the city, he came to pleasant fields. Then, after
wading awhile through the sunlit grain, he followed a
shady brook and entered the wood.

"It 's pleasant here," he thought. "I wonder why
mother did n't get a cottage out here in the country instead of living in the noisy city."

"Could n't," croaked a voice close by.

Tom started. There was nobody near but frogs and
crickets. Besides, as he had not spoken aloud, of course
it could not be in answer to him. Still, he wondered
what in the world the voice could be, and why it sounded
like "could n't."

"It certainly did sound so. Maybe she could n't, after
all," thought Tom; "but *why* could n't she, I wonder?"

"No-one-to-help," said something, as it jumped with a
splash into the water.

"I do wonder what that was!" exclaimed Tom, aloud;
"there 's nobody here, that 's certain. Oh, it must have

been a toad! Queer, though, how very much it sounded like 'no-one-to-help'! Poor mother! I don't help her much, I know. Pshaw! what if I *do* love her, I 'm not the least bit of use, for I never know what to start about doing. What in all botheration makes me so lazy! Heigh-ho!" and Tom threw himself upon the grass, an image of despair. 'He 'll never amount to anything,' the King said. Now, what *did* he mean by that?"

"Dilly, dally!" said another mysterious voice, speaking far up among the branches overhead.

Tom was getting used to it. He just lifted his eyebrows a little and wondered what bird that was. In a moment he found himself puzzling over the strange words.

"'Dilly, dally,' it said, I declare. Oh dear! It 's too bad to have to hear such things all the time. And then, there 's the King's ugly speech; a fellow is n't agoing to stand everything!"

He rested his elbows upon his knees, holding his face between his hands; and, although he felt very wretched, he could n't help wondering whether the daisies crowding in his shadow did n't think it was growing late. They certainly nodded as if they felt sleepy.

Suddenly his hat, which had tumbled from his head and now lay near him, began to twitch strangely.

"Pshaw!" almost sobbed Tom, "what 's coming now, I wonder?"

"I am," said a piping voice.

"Where are you?" he asked, trembling.

"Here. Under your hat. Lift it off."

While Tom was wondering whether to obey or not, the

hat fell over, and out came a fairy, all shining with green and gold,—a funny little creature with a sprightly air. Her eyes sparkled like diamonds.

"What troubles you, Master Tom?" asked the fairy.

"So she knows my name!" thought the puzzled youth; "well, that's queerer than anything! I've always heard that these woods were full of fairies; but I never saw one before. I wonder why I'm not more frightened."

"Did you hear me?" piped the little visitor.

"Did you speak? Oh—yes—ma'am—certainly, I heard plainly enough."

"Well, what troubles you?"

He looked sharply at the fairy. Yes, her little face was kind. He would tell her all.

"I wonder what your name is?" he said, by way of a beginning.

"It's Setalit," said the fairy. "In mortal language that means 'come-to-the-point.' Now be quick! — if you can. I sha'n't stay long."

"Why?" asked Tom, quite astonished.

"Because I cannot. That's enough. If you wish me to help you, you must promptly tell me your trouble."

"Oh!" said Tom, wondering where to begin.

"Are you lame? Are you sick? Are you blind, deaf, or dumb?" she asked, briskly.

"Oh no," he replied, "nothing like that. Only I don't know what to make of things. Everything in this world puzzles me so, and I can't ever make up my mind what to do."

"Well," said Setalit, "perhaps I can help you a little."

"Can you?" he exclaimed. "Now I wonder how in the world such a little mite as you ever—"

"Don't wonder so much," squeaked the fairy, impatiently, "but ask me frankly what I can do?"

"I 'm going to," said Tom.

"Going to!" she echoed. "What miserable creatures you mortals are! How could we ever get our gossamers spun if we always were going to do a thing, and never doing it! Now listen. I 'm a very wise fairy, if I *am* small; I can tell you how to accomplish anything you please. Don't you want to be good, famous, and rich?"

"Certainly I do," answered Tom, startled into making a prompt reply.

"Very well," she responded, quite pleased. "If you always knew your own mind as decidedly as that, they would n't call you 'Wondering Tom.' It 's an ugly name, Master Mortal. If I were you (may Titania pardon the dreadful supposition!)—if I were you, I 'd wonder less and work more."

"I wonder if I could n't!" said Tom, half convinced.

"There you go again!" screeched the fairy, stamping her tiny foot. "You 're not worth talking to. I shall leave you."

"She 's fading away," cried Tom. "O fairy, good fairy, please come back! You promised to tell me how to become good and famous and rich!"

Once more she stood before him, looking brighter and fresher than ever.

"You 're a noisy mortal," she said, nodding pleasantly at Tom. "I thought for an instant that it was thunder-

ing, but it was only you, calling. I've a very little while
to stay, but you shall have one more chance of obtaining
everything you wish. Now, sir, be careful! I'll answer
you any three questions you may choose to put to me"; and
Setalit sat down on a toadstool, and looked very profound.

"Only three?" asked Tom, anxiously.

"Only three."

"Why can't you give me a dozen? There's so much
that one wishes to know in this world."

"Because I cannot," said the fairy, firmly.

"But it's so hard to put everything into such a few
questions! I don't know what in the world to decide upon.
What do *you* think I ought to ask?"

"Consult the dearest wishes of your heart," answered
Setalit, "for there is the truest wisdom."

"Ah, well. Let me think," pursued Tom, with great deliberation. "I want to be wise, of course, and good, and
very rich,—and I want mother to be the same,—and,
good fairy, if you would n't mind it, little Wisk to be the
same too. And dear me!—it's hard to put everything into
such a few questions. Let me see. First, I suppose I ought
to learn how to become immensely rich, right off, and then
I can give mother and Wisk everything they want; so, good
Setalit, here's my first question, How can I grow rich, *very*
rich, in — in one week?"

The fairy shook her head.

"I would answer you, Master Tom, with great pleasure,"
she said, "but this is number FOUR. You have already
asked your three questions." And she turned into a green
frog and jumped away, chuckling.

Tom rubbed his eyes and sat up straight. Had he been dreaming?

"I'm a fool!" he cried.

All the trees nodded, and their branches seemed to be having great fun among themselves.

"A *big* fool!" he insisted.

The leaves fairly tittered.

"Did n't old Katy, the apple-woman, call me a goose only this morning?" he continued, growing very angry with himself.

"Katy did," assented a voice from among the bushes.

"Katy did n't!" contradicted another.

"Katy did!"

"Katy did n't!"

Tom laughed bitterly.

"Ha! ha! Fight it out among yourselves, old fellows. I may have been asleep; but, anyhow, I 've been a fool!"

"Ooo—!" echoed a solemn voice above him.

Tom looked up, and in the hollow of an old tree he saw a great blinking owl.

"Hallo, old Goggle-eyes! You 're having something to say, too, are you?"

The owl shifted his position, and stared at Tom an instant. Then, as if the sight of so ridiculous a fellow was too much for him, he shut his eyes with a loud "T'whit!" that made Tom jump.

All these things set the poor boy to thinking in earnest. The words of Setalit were ringing in his ears, "*If I were you, I 'd wonder less and work more.*" Going back through the wood across the brook, and over the lots, he pondered and pondered over the day's events, but with new resolution in his soul. And the result of all his pondering was that, as he entered the city gate, he snapped his fingers, saying, "The King's words shall never come true! Wondering Tom is going to work at last!"

———

THREE years passed away.

"Little Wisk" grew to be quite a big girl; but nobody thought of calling her by any other name. She was so lithe and quick, so rosy, fresh, and sparkling, and so tender and true withal, that she was Little Wisk as a matter of course.

One chilly November afternoon she missed old Katy, the old apple-woman, from her accustomed place at the street corner.

"She must be ill," thought little Wisk. "Perhaps she has no one to help her."

With some persons, to think is to act. Wisk stepped into a neighboring cobbler's shop.

"Mr. Wacksend, do you know where the old apple-woman lives?"

"No," said the cobbler, gruffly. "Shut the door when you go out."

Little Wisk looked at him as he sat upon his bench, pegging away at his work.

"Poor man!" she said to herself, "pushing the awl through that thick leather makes him press his lips tight together, and I suppose pressing his lips so tight, day after day, makes him cross. I'll try the butcher."

She ran into the next shop.

"Mr. Butcher, do you know where the old apple-woman lives?"

"Well," said the butcher, pausing to wipe his cleaver on his big apron, "she does n't exactly *live* anywhere. But, as the poor thing has neither kith nor kin to help her, why, for the past year or so I 've just let her tumble herself in under a shed in my yard yonder. She 's got an old chopping-bench for a table, and a pile of straw for a bed, and that 's all her housekeeping."

"And does n't she have anything to eat but apples?" asked Wisk, much distressed.

"Bless your simple heart!" said the butcher, laughing, "she can't afford to eat her apples. No, no. She keeps the breath in her body mostly with black bread and scraps."

"Scraps?"

"Yes, meat-scraps. I save 'em for her out of the trimmin's. But what are you wantin' of her so particular? Did you come to invite her to court?"

"I 'd like to see her for a moment," said Wisk, shrinking from his coarse laugh.

"Well," answered the butcher, beginning to chop again, "the surest way of seeing her is to go to the corner and buy an apple."

"But she is n't there."

"Not there? That 's uncommon. Well,"—pointing back over his shoulder with his cleaver,—"go down the alley here, alongside the shop; steer clear of old Beppo in his kennel, he 's ugly sometimes; then go past the pigsties and the skin-heaps, and cross over by the cattle-stalls;

and right back of them, a little beyond, is the shed. May-be she 's lying there sick ; like enough, poor thing !"

Little Wisk followed the directions, as she picked her way carefully through the great bleak cattle-yard, think-ing, as she went, that killing lambs did n't always make a man so very wicked, after all. .

Reaching the shed, she found the poor old apple-woman, moaning and bent nearly double with rheumatism.

"'I 'M SORRY YOU ARE NOT WELL, GOODY,' SAID LITTLE WISK."

" I 'm sorry you are not well, Goody," said Little Wisk. " We missed you, you know. What can I do for you ? "

" Bless your bright eyes ! Did you come to see poor old Katy ? *Ough ah-h !* the pain 's killing me, child ! Oh, the Lord save us, *ough ah !* "

9

"It's too cold and damp for you in here, I'm sure."

"Ah yes, it is, dearie dear,—*ough, ough!*—cold and wet enough!"

"This old rusty stove would be nice if you had a fire in it, Goody."

"Oh, the stove, dearie! The good gentleman in the shop put it in here for me last winter. He's kept me in meat-scraps, too. Oh,—oh,—oh! (it catches me that way often, child). But, alack! I have n't a chip nor a shaving to make a bit of fire. *Oh! oh!* (the worst's in this shoulder, dearie, and 'cross the back and into this 'ere knee). Yes, cold and wet enough, so it is. *Aouch!* No use s'arching out there; you won't find nothing. Not a waste splinter of wood left, I 'll be bound, after *my* raking and scraping till I was too sick to stand up."

"I do wish I had money to buy you some, Goody," said Wisk. "I sha'n't have another silver-piece till my next birthday, but you shall have that, I promise you."

"Blessings on you for saying it, dearie; but old Katy is n't going to last till then. What with cold and hunger (the meat on the nail there 's no use, you see, if I can't cook it), and this 'ere — *ough* — *ah!* — this 'ere dreadful rheumatiz, I can't hold out much longer."

Suddenly a thought came to Wisk.

"Oh, Katy!" she exclaimed, and off she ran, past the cattle-sheds, the skin-heaps, the pigsties, the dog-kennel, up the alley, up the street, and round the corner toward the river till she came to the workshop of a ship-carpenter.

"Tom," she said, hurrying in, quite out of breath, and addressing a great strong boy who was working there, "won't you give me some shavings and chips?"

"Certainly," said Tom, straightway beginning to scrape together a big pile. "What shall we put them in?"

"Into my apron. They're for poor Katy, the apple-woman. She lives in an old shed in Slorter's cattle-yard. She's sick, Tom, and she has n't a thing to make a fire with."

"Oh, if that's it," said Tom, "we must get her up a cart-load of waste stuff, if the boss is willing."

The boss spoke up:

"Help yourself, Tom. You're the steadiest lad in the shop, and you've never asked me a favor before. Help yourself. Take along all those odds and ends in the corner yonder. Chips and shavings soon burn up."

"Much obliged to you, sir," said Tom; and he added in a lower tone to Wisk, "I'll load up and take 'em 'round to her as soon as I've done my work. You can carry your apronful now."

Wisk held up the corners of her apron while Tom filled it, laughing to see how she lifted her pretty chin so that he might pile in a "good lot," as she called it.

"There!" he exclaimed at last, "that's as much as you can manage."

"Thank you, Tom. Oh, how kind you are! I was as sure as anything that you'd know just what to do. Thank you again, Tom," and she started at once.

"Wisk!"

He had followed her to the door. When she turned back, in answer to his call, he tried to speak to her, but coughed instead.

"Did you want me, Tom?" she asked, demurely.

"Yes, Wisk. I—I wanted to say that—that I—"

"Why, what a cough you have, Tom! It 's from working so much in this windy shop. Oh, Tom, I 've just thought! If Katy had a door to her shed and a bench with a back to it, she 'd be *so* comfortable!"

"She shall have both," said Tom. "I 'll do it this very evening. It 's full moon."

"Oh, you dear, blessed Tom! Good-by."

"Wisk!"

But she was already running down the street. Tom turned back slowly. I think he was wondering, though he had really conquered that old habit. But it is so difficult, sometimes, to say just what we feel to those whom we like very much!

"First the shavings, then the chips," sang Wisk's happy heart, as she hurried along; "first the shavings, and then the chips, and then a spark from old Katy's tinder-box, and sha'n't we have a beautiful blaze!"

That night, the one-eyed dog in the butcher's yard had a hard time of it. There was the moon to be barked at; the pigs to be barked at; the sheep, the oxen, and the lambs to be barked at every time they moved in their stalls. The skin-heap, too, required a constant barking to keep it from stirring while the rats were burrowing beneath. And then there was the strange lad to be barked at, coming in twice, as he did, with a hand-cart heaped high with chips, shavings, and blocks, and again coming back with planks, hammer, and saw. And the sudden smoke from the sick woman's fire; ah, how it bothered old Beppo!

He had lived long in the yard, and remembered well

how the high chimney had stood there for years and
years,—all that was left of a burned-down factory,—
and how the shed had been built up around it as if to
keep it from tumbling. For months past it had been a
quiet, well-behaved chimney; but now to see smoke rushing out of it at such a rate, bound straight for that irri-
tating moon, was really too much to stand. So Beppo
barked and barked; and Tom hammered and hammered;
and old Katy, warm at last, curled herself up in the
straw, saying over and over again, "How nice it will be!
How nice it will be!"

———

YEARS passed on. One day, the King and his court
came riding down that same city again. Suddenly his
Majesty, grown older now, halted before a boat-builder's
shop, and asked:

"Who is that busy fellow, yonder?"

"Where, your most prodigal Majesty?" asked the Prime
Minister in return.

"In the shop. Yesterday this same young fellow and
his man were busy out on the docks. He works with
a will, that fellow. I must set him at the royal ships."

"The royal ships!" echoed the Prime Minister, "your
most overwhelming Majesty; why, that is a fortune for
any man!"

"I know it. Why not?" said the King. "What is his
name?"

The Prime Minister could not say. And again, as on
that day long before, the question traveled through the

9*

"'THOMAS REDDY, YOUR MAJESTY.'"

grandees of the court, until it reached the Chief-Cook-and-Bottle-Washer, and the Chief-Cook-and-Bottle-Washer asked a pretty young woman named Wisk, who chanced to be coming out of the shop.

"He 's a master-builder," replied Wisk, blushing.

"But what 's his name?" repeated the Chief-Cook-and-Bottle-Washer.

"He used to be called Wondering Tom," she answered; "but now we all call him by his real name, Thomas Reddy."

"Thomas Reddy!" shouted the Chief-Cook-and-Bottle-Washer. "Thomas Reddy!" cried the Royal Rat-Catcher.

And, in fact, "Thomas Reddy!" was called so often and so loudly along the line before it reached the only officer who could venture to speak to the King, that the master-builder, with a keen eye to business, threw down his tools and came out of the shop.

"Oh, Tom! Again the King wishes to speak with you," said Little Wisk.

They took each other by the hand, and together walked toward his Majesty.

"Behold!" said the King, "we have found the finest young workman in our realms! Let preparations be made at once for proclaiming him Royal Ship-Builder! What do they call you, young man? I 've lost the name."

"Thomas Reddy, your Majesty," he answered, his eye sparkling with grateful joy.

"And who are *you*, my pretty one?"

"Oh, I 'm his wife," said the smiling Wisk.

LITTLE VEMBA BROWN

LITTLE VEMBA BROWN.

LITTLE VEMBA BROWN

VEMBA was a new name in the Brown family; and, very properly, it was given to a brand-new girl,— the sweetest, prettiest mite of a girl, in fact, that ever had come to join the Brown household. To be sure, six years before this, they had welcomed a Morris Brown nearly as small and sweet and pretty, and, later on, a Harris Brown, who began life as a baby of the very first quality; but they, both, were boys. And here was a girl! She was so new that she did not know Morris and Harris were in the house. Think of that! And if she *had* noticed them, she would not have had the slightest idea who they were. Dear me! How very well acquainted the three became after awhile! But at first, when the little girl was only a few weeks old, she was still quite a stranger to the boys, and had no other name than Miss Brown; yet she had the air of owning not only Mr. and Mrs. Brown, but all the family, and the very house they lived in. Why, the King of the Cannibal Islands himself could not have made her change countenance unless she chose to do so.

Well, there they were,— Morris Brown, aged six years,

Harris Brown, aged three, and Miss Brown of hardly any age at all. These were the Brown children.

"Dear me! a bonny little lady!" said Uncle Tom, who had come all the way from Philadelphia to take a look at the baby.

At this point of time, as he gazed at her through his spectacles, all the family crowded around; the boys, proud and happy, stood on either side of him to hear what his opinion might be.

"A bonny little lady," repeated Uncle Tom; "and now, Stephania, what are you going to call her?"

He turned so suddenly upon Mrs. Brown, in his brisk way, that it made her start.

"Dear me! I—I—don't know," she answered. "Some novel, pretty name, of course; something fanciful; but we have n't settled upon one yet."

"Why not call her Stephania, after you and me?" asked Grandmama, brightly.

"Oh, dear, no," sighed Mrs. Brown; "I 'd like some-thing not so horri—, I mean, something more fanciful than *that!*"

"Well, I declare!" exclaimed Grandmama, and she closed her lips as if resolved never to say another word about it.

"We have thought of Marjorie," remarked Mr. Brown, with a funny twinkle in his eyes, "and, ahem! two or three others,—Mabel, for instance, and Ida, and Irene, and Clara, and Jean, and Olivia; Florence, and Francesca, too, and Lily; Alice, and Elinor, and Anita, and Jessie, and Dora, and Isabel, and Bertha, and Louise, and Cardace, and Alma; but Stephania condemns every one of them as too plain or too hackneyed. The fact is, all the pretty names are used up."

"You might name her Chestnut," said Morris, musingly. "There are three of us, and three is an awful lot."

Just then the wind howled dismally; sere and yellow leaves whirled past the windows.

"Goodness, what weather!" exclaimed Grandmama. "Bleak even for November—is n't it?"

"Here 's sunshine, though," murmured Mrs. Brown, cheerily. "You 're a 'ittle pessus bit of booful sunshine, so you is, even if you *is* a poor 'itty 'Vember baby!" and she fell to kissing Miss Brown in the most rapturous manner.

"Ha! there it is!" cried Uncle Tom. "Vemba 's her name. Her mother has said it. Let us call her Vemba!"

Every one laughed, but Uncle Tom was in earnest; besides, he had to take the afternoon train back to Philadelphia,—and you know how they always rush matters through in Philadelphia.

"It 's a good name, and new," he said, nodding his head in a rotary way that somehow took in Mr. Brown, Mrs. Brown, Grandma Brown, Morris Brown, Harris Brown, and Miss Brown. "It 's a good name. Think it over. I must be off!"

"Vemba, from November?" cried Grandma. "What a bleak name! Do you want the poor child to be a shadow on the house?" and the dear old lady flourished her knitting as she spoke.

Whether it was the gleam of the long needles, or Uncle

Tom's frantic but slow way of putting on his coat,—or whether Miss Brown, catching Grandma Brown's words, had suddenly resolved to show them that she had n't the slightest intention in the world of being a shadow on the house, I do not know. But certain it is she smiled,— smiled the brightest, sunniest little smile you can imagine.

All the family were delighted. The boys shouted, Papa laughed, Mama laughed, Uncle Tom laughed, and Grandma exclaimed, " Well, I never ! "

" She 's answered you, Grandma ! " cried Uncle Tom, bending down with only one sleeve of his overcoat on,— and actually kissing the baby,—" she has answered you. Ha, ha ! No clouds about *her ;* you see she 's a sunshine-girl. Well, good-by, little Vemba ! Good-by, all," and he was out of the room and on his way to the train before the baby had time to blink.

Well, to make a long story short, the more they thought about the new name, the better they liked it. Besides, Morris and Harris, who adored Uncle Tom, would hear of no other. Papa declared it was not " half bad," and even Mama admitted that at least it was not commonplace. Meanwhile, the baby fell into a pleasant sleep.

When she awoke her name was Vemba Brown.

That was five years ago, this November, and now every one says that of all the sweet, sunny, bright little girls in New York, Vemba Brown is the sunniest, brightest, and sweetest. She is now thoroughly acquainted with Morris and Harris ; and as for Uncle Tom—well, you should have heard her laugh the other day when that gentleman told the wee maiden that bleak November would soon

be here, and then everybody would shiver and sneeze —
So!—and you should have seen her throw her arms around
his neck and kiss him when that same day he gave her a
beautiful new walking-suit and a soft white muff to keep
her little hands warm!

And oh, you should have seen, besides, what the little
maid found waiting for her when she went down to breakfast on that happy birthday! A gift from Mama, and another from Papa. One of the gifts was very quiet, for it
held a secret; the other at first was just a little noisy, and
he soon told Vemba all he knew.

WAITING FOR VEMBA!

THE CROW-CHILD

CORA AND RUKY.

MIDWAY between a certain blue lake and a deep forest there once stood a cottage, called by its owner "The Rookery."

The forest shut out the sunlight and scowled upon the ground, breaking with shadows every ray that fell, until only a few little pieces lay scattered about. But the broad lake invited all the rays to come and rest upon her, so that sometimes she shone from shore to shore, and the sun winked and blinked above her, as though dazzled by his own reflection. The cottage, which was very small, had sunny windows and dark windows. Only from the roof could you see the mountains beyond, where the light crept up in the morning and down in the evening, turning all the brooks into living silver as it passed.

But something brighter than sunshine used often to look from the cottage into the forest, and something even more gloomy than shadows often glowered from its windows upon the sunny lake. One was the face of little Ruky Lynn; and the other was his sister's when she felt angry or ill-tempered.

They were orphans, Cora and Ruky, living alone in the cottage with an old uncle. Cora — or "Cor," as Ruky called her — was nearly sixteen years old, but her brother had seen the forest turn yellow only four times. She was, therefore, almost mother and sister in one. The little fellow was her companion night and day. Together they ate and slept, and — when Cora was not at work in the cottage — together they rambled in the wood, or floated in their little skiff upon the lake.

Ruky had bright, dark eyes, and the glossy blackness of his hair made his cheeks look even rosier than they were. He had funny ways for a boy, Cora thought. The quick, bird-like jerks of his raven-black head, his stately baby gait, and his habit of pecking at his food, as she called it, often made his sister laugh. Young as he was, the little fellow had learned to mount to the top of a low-branching tree near the cottage, though he could not always get down alone. Sometimes when, perched in the thick foliage, he would scream, "Cor! Cor! Come, help me down!" his sister would answer, as she ran out laughing, "Yes, little Crow! I'm coming."

Perhaps it was because he reminded her of a crow that Cora called him her little bird. This was when she was good-natured and willing to let him see how much she loved him. But in her cloudy moments, as the uncle called them, Cora was another girl. Everything seemed ugly to her, or out of tune. Even Ruky was a trial; and, instead of giving him a kind word, she would scold and grumble until he would steal from the cottage door, and, jumping lightly from the door-step, seek the shelter of his tree. Once safely perched among its branches he knew she would finish her work, forget her ill-humor, and be quite ready, when he cried "Cor! Cor!" to come from the cottage with a cheery, "Yes, little Crow! I 'm coming! I 'm coming!"

No one could help loving Ruky, with his quick, affectionate ways; and it seemed that Ruky, in turn, could not help loving every person and thing around him. He loved his silent old uncle, the bright lake, the cool forest,

THE HOME OF CORA AND RUKY.

and even his little china cup with red berries painted upon it. But more than all, Ruky loved his golden-haired sister, and the great dog, who would plunge into the lake at the mere pointing of his chubby little finger. In fact, that finger and the commanding baby voice were "law" to Nep at any time.

Nep and Ruky often talked together, and though one used barks and the other words, there was a perfect understanding between them. Woe to the straggler that dared to rouse Nep's wrath, and woe to the bird or rabbit that ventured too near!—those great teeth snapped at their prey

10*

without even the warning of a growl. But Ruky could safely pull Nep's ears or his tail, or climb his great shaggy back, or even snatch away the untasted bone. Still, as I said before, every one loved the child; so, of course, Nep was no exception.

One day Ruky's "Cor! Cor!" had sounded oftener than usual. His rosy face had bent saucily to kiss Cora's up-turned forehead, as she raised her arms to lift him from the tree; but the sparkle in his dark eyes had seemed to kindle so much mischief in him that his sister's patience became fairly exhausted.

" Has Cor nothing to do but to wait upon *you?*" she cried, "and nothing to listen to but your noise and your racket? You shall go to bed early to-day, and then I shall have some peace."

" No, no, Cor. Please let Ruky wait till the stars come. Ruky wants to see the stars."

" Hush! Ruky is bad. He shall have a whipping when Uncle comes back from town."

Nep growled.

" Ha! ha!" laughed Ruky, jerking his head saucily from side to side; " Nep says 'No!'"

Nep was shut out of the cottage for his pains, and poor Ruky was undressed, with many a hasty jerk and pull.

" You hurt, Cor!" he said, plaintively. " I 'm going to take off my shoes my own self."

" No, you 're not," cried Cora, almost shaking him; and when he cried she called him naughty, and said if he did not stop he should have no supper. This made him cry all the more, and Cora, feeling in her angry mood that he deserved severe punishment, threw away his supper and put him to bed. Then all that could be heard were Ruky's low sobs and the snappish clicks of Cora's needles, as she sat knitting, with her back to him.

He could not sleep, for his eyelids were scalded with tears, and his plaintive "Cor! Cor!" had reached his sister's ears in vain. She never once looked up from those gleaming knitting-needles, nor even gave him his good-night kiss.

It grew late. The uncle did not return. At last Cora, sulky and weary, locked the cottage door, blew out her candle, and lay down beside her brother.

The poor little fellow tried to win a forgiving word, but she was too ill-natured to grant it. In vain he whispered, "Cor, Cor!" He even touched her hand over and over again with his lips, hoping she would turn toward him, and, with a loving kiss, murmur, as usual, "Good night, little bird."

Instead of this, she jerked her arm angrily away, saying:

"Oh, stop your pecking and go to sleep! I wish you were a crow in earnest, and then I 'd have some peace."

After this, Ruky was silent. His heart drooped within him as he wondered what this "peace" was that his sister wished for so often, and why he must go away before it could come to her.

Soon, Cora, who had rejoiced in the sudden calm, heard a strange fluttering. In an instant she saw by the starlight a dark object circle once or twice in the air above her, then dart suddenly through the open window.

Astonished that Ruky had not shouted with delight at the strange visitor, or else clung to her neck in fear, she turned to see if he had fallen asleep.

No wonder that she started up, horror-stricken,—Ruky was not there !

His empty place was still warm; perhaps he had slid softly from the bed. With trembling haste she lighted the candle, and peered into every corner. The boy was not to be found !

Then those fearful words rang in her ears:

"*I wish you were a crow in earnest !*"

Cora rushed to the door, and, with straining gaze, looked out into the still night.

"Ruky ! Ruky !" she screamed.

There was a slight stir in the low-growing tree.

"Ruky, darling, come back !"

"Caw, caw !" answered a harsh voice from the tree. Something black seemed to spin out of it, and then, in great sweeping circles, sailed upward, until finally it settled upon one of the loftiest trees in the forest.

"Caw, caw !" it screamed, fiercely.

The girl shuddered, but, with outstretched arms, cried out :

"Oh, Ruky, if it is *you*, come back to poor Cor !"

"Caw, caw !" mocked hundreds of voices, as a shadow like a thunder-cloud rose in the air. It was an immense flock of crows. She could distinguish them plainly in the starlight, circling higher and higher, then lower and lower, until, with their harsh "Caw, caw !" they sailed far off into the night.

"Oh, Ruky, answer me !" she cried.

Nep growled, the forest trees whispered softly together, and the lake, twinkling with stars, sang a lullaby as it lifted

its weary little waves upon the shore: there was no other
sound.

It seemed that daylight never would come; but at last
the trees turned slowly from black to green, and the lake
put out its stars, one by one, and waited for the new day.

Cora, who had been wandering restlessly in every direction, now went weeping into the cottage. " Poor boy !" she
sobbed; " he had no supper." Then she scattered bread-
crumbs near the doorway, hoping that Ruky would come
for them; but only a few timid little songsters hovered
about, and, while Cora wept, picked up the food daintily,
as though it burned their bills. When she reached forth
her hand, though there were no crows among them, and
called " Ruky ! Ruky !" they scattered and flew away in
an instant.

Next she went to the steep-roofed barn, and, bringing
out an apronful of grain, scattered it all around his favorite
tree. Before long, to her great joy, a flock of crows came
by. They spied the grain, and soon were busily picking it
up with their short, feathered bills. One even came near
the mound where she sat. Unable to restrain herself
longer, she fell upon her knees with an imploring cry:

" Oh, Ruky ! is this you ?"

Instantly the entire flock set up an angry " caw," and,
surrounding the crow, who was hopping closer and closer to
Cora, hurried him off, until they all looked like mere specks
against the summer sky.

Every day, rain or shine, she scattered the grain, trembl-
ling with dread lest Nep should leap among the hungry
crows, and perhaps kill her " little bird" first. But Nep

"'OH, RUKY! IS THIS YOU?'"

knew better; he never stirred when the noisy crowd settled around the cottage, excepting once, when one of them
pounced upon his back. Then he started up, wagging his
tail, and barking with uproarious delight. The crow flew
off in a flutter, and did not venture near him again.

Poor Cora felt sure that this could be no other than Ruky. Oh, if she only could have caught him then ! Perhaps with kisses and prayers she might have won him back to Ruky's shape; but now the chance was lost.

There was no one to help her ; for the nearest neighbor dwelt miles away, and her uncle had not yet returned.

After awhile she remembered the little cup, and, filling it with grain, stood it upon a grassy mound. When the crows came, they fought and struggled for its contents with many an angry cry. One of them made no effort to seize the grain. He was content to peck at the berries painted upon its sides, as he hopped joyfully around it again and again. Nep lay very quiet. Only the tip of his tail twitched with an eager, wistful motion. But Cora sprang joyfully toward the bird.

"It *is* Ruky !" she cried, striving to catch it.

Alas ! the cup lay shattered beneath her hand, as, with a taunting " caw, caw," the crow joined its fellows and flew away.

Next, gunners came. They were looking for other birds; but they hated the crows, Cora knew, and she trembled for Ruky. She heard the sharp crack of fowling-pieces in the forest, and shuddered whenever Nep, pricking up his ears, darted with an angry howl in the direction of the sound. She knew, too, that her uncle had set traps for the crows, and it seemed to her that the whole world was against the poor birds, plotting their destruction.

Time flew by. The leaves seemed to flash into bright colors and fall off almost in a day. Frost and snow came. Still the uncle had not returned, or, if he had, she did not

"A TERRIBLE NIGHT OF WIND AND STORM."

know it. Her brain was bewildered. She knew not whether she ate or slept. Only the terrible firing reached her ears, or that living black cloud came and went with its ceaseless "caw."

At last, during a terrible night of wind and storm, Cora felt that she must go forth and seek her poor bird.

"Perhaps he is freezing—dying!" she cried, springing frantically from the bed, and casting her long cloak over her night-dress.

In a moment, she was trudging barefooted through the snow. It was so deep she could hardly walk, and the sleet was driving into her face; still she kept on, though her numbed feet seemed hardly to belong to her. All the way she was praying in her heart; promising never, never to be passionate again, if she only could find her bird — not Ruky the boy, but whatever he might be. She was willing to accept her punishment. Soon a faint cry reached her ear. With eager haste, she peered into every fold of the drifted snow. A black object caught her eye. It was a poor storm-beaten crow, lying there benumbed and stiff.

For Ruky's sake she folded it closely to her bosom, and plodded back to the cottage. The fire cast a rosy light on its glossy wing as she entered, but the poor thing did not stir. Softly stroking and warming it, she wrapped the frozen bird in soft flannel and blew into its open mouth. Soon, to her great relief, it revived, and even swallowed a few grains of wheat.

Cold and weary, she cast herself upon the bed, still folding the bird to her heart. "It may be Ruky! It is all I ask," she sobbed. "I dare not ask for more."

"JUST TWO HOURS."

Suddenly she felt a peculiar stirring. The crow seemed
to grow larger. Then, in the dim light, she felt its feathers
pressing lightly against her cheek. Next, something soft
and warm wound itself tenderly about her neck, and she
heard a sweet voice saying:

"Don't cry, Cor,—I 'll be good."

She started up. It was, indeed, her own darling! The starlight shone into the room. Lighting her candle, she looked at the clock.

It was just two hours since she had uttered those cruel words! Sobbing, she asked:

"Have I been asleep, Ruky, dear?"

"I don't know, Cor. Do people cry when they're asleep?"

"Sometimes, Ruky," clasping him very close.

"Then you have been asleep. But Cor, please don't let Uncle whip Ruky."

"No, no, my little bird—I mean, my brother. Good night, darling!"

"Good night."

TRAPPER JOE

TRAPPER JOE STOOD ON THE EDGE OF THE TIMBER-LAND LISTENING
TO "HE DID N'T KNOW WHAT." (PAGE 173.)

How strange it all seemed to little Winifred! One
year ago, or, as she reckoned it, one snow-time and one
flower-time ago, she was living in Boston, and now she
was in the wilds of Colorado. It was a great change —
this going from comfort and luxury to a place where comfort was hard to find, and luxury not to be thought of;
where they had a log-hut instead of a house, and a pig in
place of a poodle. But, on the whole, she enjoyed it. Her
father was better, and that was what they came for. The
doctor had said Colorado air would cure him. And, though
her young Mother often looked tired and troubled, she
certainly never used to break forth into happy bits of song
when Father was ill in bed, as she did now that he was
able to help cut down trees in the forest. Besides, who
ever saw in Boston such beautiful blue flowers and such
flaming red blossoms? And what was the frog-pond com-
pared with these streams that now, in the springtime,
came rushing through the woods—silently sometimes, and
sometimes so noisily that, if it were not for their sparkle
when they passed the open, sunny places, and the playful

way they had of running into every chink along the banks, one would think they were angry? Yes, on the whole, Winifred liked Colorado; and so did her little brother Nat; though, if you had told him Boston was just around the corner, he would have started to run there without waiting to put on his cap.

A little mite of a fellow Nat was, full of good nature and sunshine. Although he thought himself quite a big boy, as he strutted about in his home-made jacket and trousers, one thing could sorely trouble him — and that was to be away from Mother, even for an hour. There was something in Mother's way of singing, Mother's way of kissing hurt little heads and fingers, Mother's way of sprinkling sugar upon bread, and Mother's way of rocking tired little boys, that Nat approved of most heartily. He loved his father, too, and thought him the most powerful woodcutter that ever swung an ax, though really the poor man had to stop and rest at nearly every stroke.

See these two children now trudging toward the shallow bend of the little river near by, quite intent upon the launching and sailing of a tiny sloop that Father had made for Nat on the evening before, warranting only that she would float. This she did, and reared her one sail most gallantly. But alas! inspired by the current she sailed too well. It required the restraining efforts of both children to keep her near shore; and when at last Winnie remarked in cold scorn that she did n't see much fun in sailing a boat that had to be pulled back all the time, Nat and she promptly decided to try some other kind of sport.

Father's big rowboat was moored close by, and why not

get into it and set it a-rocking? Father and Mother both had laughed the other day to see them do this — so of course there could be no harm in it.

But when they had climbed into the rowboat they found it too hot and sunny. At least Winnie said it was so.

"NOT MUCH FUN IN SAILING A BOAT THAT HAD TO BE PULLED BACK
ALL THE TIME."

"Let's try the canoe," she added, in a sprightly way. "I'm sure Papa would let us just sit in it."

"Course he would," responded Nat, promptly beginning to climb out of the boat as he spoke.

The canoe was tied to a stake a little farther downstream, where the river grew narrow, and the current was much stronger. It was made of bark, and was pointed at both ends. Now that the stream was swollen and flowing fast, it was fine fun to sit together in the middle and "get bounced about," as Winnie said.

11*

"You get in first, because you 're the littlest," said Winnie, holding her dress tightly away from the plashing water with one hand, and pulling the boat close to the shore with the other.

"No, *you* get in first, 'cause you 'm a girl," said Nat. "I don't want any helpin'. I 'm going to take off my toos and 'tockies first, 'cause Mama said I might."

Nat could say "shoes and stockings" quite plainly when he chose, but everybody said "toos and 'tockies" to him; so he looked upon these words, and many other crooked ones, as a sort of language of Nat, which all the world would speak if they only knew how.

In at last,— both of them,— and a fine rocking they had. The bushes and trees threw cool shadows over the canoe, and the birds sang, and the blue sky peeped down at them through little openings overhead, and, altogether, with the plashing water and the birds and pleasant murmur of insects, it was almost like Mother's rocking and singing.

At first they talked and laughed softly. Then they listened. Then they talked a very little; then they listened again, lying on the rushes in the bottom of the canoe. Then they ceased talking, and watched the branches waving overhead; and, at last, they both fell sound asleep.

This was early in the forenoon. Mother was very busy in the cabin, sweeping the room, making the beds, heating the oven, and doing a dozen other things. At last she took a plate of crumbs, and went out to feed the chickens.

"Winnie! Nat!" she called, as she stepped out upon the clean, rough door-stone. "Come, feed the chickens!"

Then she added, in a surprised way, to herself: "Why, where in the world can those children be? They must have stopped at the new clearing to see their father."

At dinner-time, she blew the big tin horn that hung by the door, and soon her husband came home alone, hungry and tired.

"Oh, you little witches!" laughed the mother, without looking up from her task of bread-cutting. "How could you stay away so long from Mama? Tired, Frank?"

"Yes, very. But what do you mean? Where *are* the youngsters?"

She looked up now, exclaiming in a frightened voice, as she ran out past her husband: "Oh, Frank! I've not seen them for two or three hours. I thought they were with you. They surely would

"'OH, FRANK! FRANK! THE
CANOE IS GONE!'"

n't have played all this time with the little sloop!"

The father, who was indeed very weary, and not at all alarmed, sat quietly awaiting her return. But when, in a few moments, she rushed in screaming: "Oh, Frank! Frank! the canoe is gone!" he sprang up, and together they ran toward the stream.

All that long, terrible day, and the next, they searched. They followed the stream, and at last found the canoe — but it was empty! In vain the father and mother and their only neighbor wandered through the forest in every direction, calling: "Winnie! Winnie! Nat! Nat!" In vain the father and the neighbor took their boats and explored the stream for miles and miles — no trace could be found of the poor little creatures who, full of life and joy, had so lately jumped into their father's canoe to "be bounced about."

Where were they? Alas! they themselves did not know. They only knew that they had been wakened suddenly by a great thump, and that when they sprang out of the canoe, and started to go home, everything was different. There was no foot-path, no clearing where trees had been cut down, no sound of Father's ax near by, nor of Mother's song — and the stream was rushing on very angrily over its sandy bed. The canoe, which had broken loose and, borne on by the current, had drifted away with them nearly three miles from the stake, was wedged between two great stones when they jumped out of it; but now it was gone — the waters had taken it away. After a while, in their distracted wanderings, they could not even find the stream, though it seemed to be roaring in every direction around them.

Now they were in the depths of the forest, wandering about, tired, hungry and frightened. That night they cried themselves to sleep in each other's arms under the black trees; and, as the wind moaned through the branches, Winnie had prayed God to save them from the wolves, and little Nat had screamed, "Papa! Mama!" sobbing as if his heart would break.

In the morning all they could find to eat was a few sweet red berries that grew close to the ground.

Every hour the poor children grew fainter, and, at last, Nat could n't walk at all.

"I 'm too tired and sick," he said, "and my feets all tut. My toos and 'tockies is in the boat. O Winnie! Winnie!" he would cry, with a great sob, "why *don't* Mama 'n' Papa come? Oh, if Mama 'd only come and bring us some bread!"

"Don't cry, dear — don't cry," Winnie would say over and over again. "I 'll find some more red berries soon; and God will show us the way home. I *know* he will. Only don't cry, Nat, because it takes away all my courage."

"What?" asked Nat, looking wildly at her as if he thought courage was something they could eat.

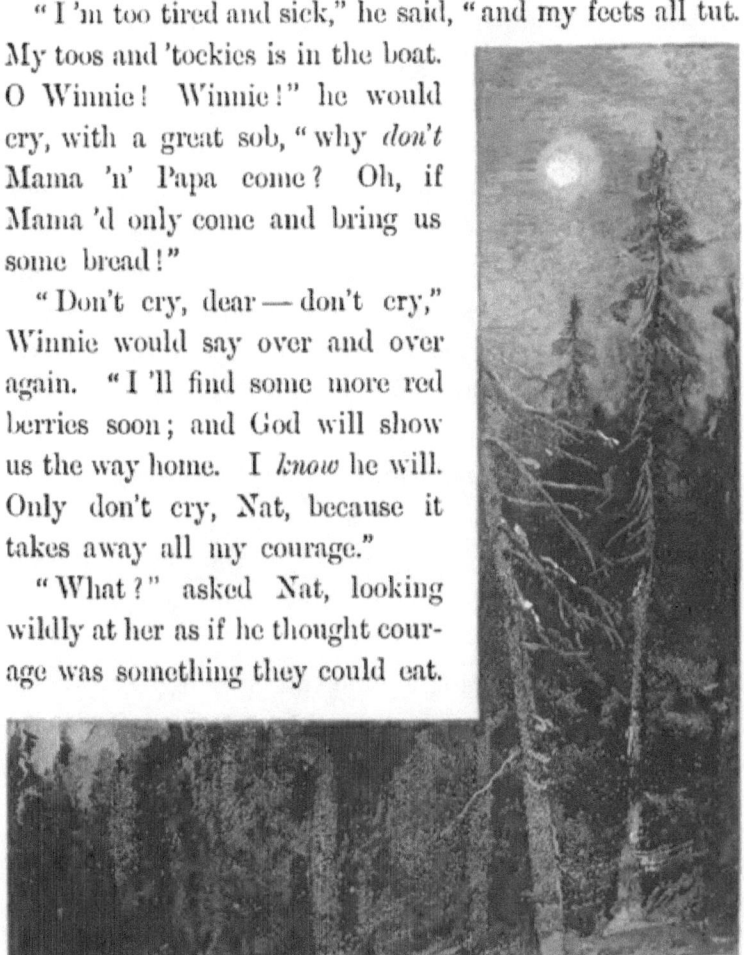

"All my courage, Nat." And then, after searching in vain for more red berries, she would moan: "Dear Father in Heaven, I can't find anything more for Nat to eat. Oh, *please* show us the way home!"

Often she would tie her handkerchief high upon some sapling, and, charging Nat on no account to "move a single inch, dear," she would place him down by the tree, and then press through the thicket and stumble over fallen boughs in the vain hope of spying a foot-path or at least the gleam of the noisy stream. Never once, however, did she lose sight of the handkerchief that hung limp and spiritless above Nat's head.

In vain. There was no path; only the wilderness and the growing darkness in every direction; not a berry anywhere. Returning to her brother, and stroking his restless little hands and whispering cheery words, she would sink to the ground, and sob, in spite of herself.

What was that quick sound coming toward them? The underbrush was so thick Winnie could not see what caused it, but she held her breath in terror, thinking of wolves and Indians, for there were many of both, she knew, lurking about in these great forests.

The sound ceased for a moment. Seizing Nat in her arms, she made one more frantic effort to find her way to the stream, then, seeing a strange look in the poor little face when she put him down to take a firmer hold, she screamed:

"Nat! Nat! Don't look so! Speak to Winnie!"

"Hello, there!" shouted a voice through the underbrush, and in another instant a tall, keen-faced man came stamping and breaking his way through the bushes.

" Hello, there! What on airth 's up now? Ef old Joe hain't come upon queer game this time. Two sick youngsters — an' ef they ain't a-starving! Here, you young uns, eat some uv this 'ere, and give an account uv yourselves."

With these words, he drew from a leather pouch at his side, a couple of crackers.

The children clutched at them frantically.

" Hold up! Not so sharp!" he said; " you must have a little at a time for an hour yet. Here, sis, give me the little one — I 'll feed him; and as for you, jest see that you don't more 'n *nibble!*"

" Oh, give me a drink!" cried Winnie, swallowing the cracker in two bites, and for an instant even forgetting Nat.

The man pulled a canteen or flat thin flask from his belt and gave her a swallow of water; then he hastened to moisten Nat's lips and feed him crumb after crumb of the broken cracker.

"Another day," he muttered to himself, as he gently fed the boy and smoothed back the tangled yellow hair from the pale little face, — " another day, and he 'd 'a' been past mendin'."

Winnie looked up quickly.

" Is he going to die?" she asked.

" Not he," said the man; " he 'll come through right end up yet. He 's got a fever on him, but we 'll soon knock that under. How 'd you get here, little gal?"

Winnie told her story, all the while feeling a glad certainty at her heart that their troubles were over.

The strange man carried a gun, and he had a big pistol,

and a knife at the back of his belt. He looked very fierce,
too, yet she knew he would not harm her. She had seen
many a trapper since she had come to the West, and, besides, she felt almost sure he was the very trapper who had
been at her father's cabin a few months before, and taken
supper, warming himself by the big fire while he told
wonderful stories about Indians and furs, and about having many a time had "fifty mile o' traps out on one
stretch." Yes, he was the very man, she believed, who had
told her parents how he had seen a bear walking one moonlight night across the very spot where their cabin now stood.

She remembered, too, that her father had told her the
next day that trappers lived by catching with traps all

sorts of wild animals, and selling their furs to the traders, and that this particular trapper had been very successful, and had great influence among the Indians — in fact, that he was "one of the big men of that country," as he said.

These thoughts running through her mind now as she told how they had been lost in the forest for two whole days, and a night, and the sight of Nat falling peacefully asleep on the trapper's shoulder, made her feel so happy that she suddenly broke forth with, "O Mr. Trapper! I can run now. Let's go right home!"

THE stars came out one by one that night, and winked and blinked at a strange figure stalking through the forest. He had a sleeping child on his arm, and yet carried his gun ready to fire at an instant's notice. Trudging on, with poor little Winnie half running beside him, he muttered to himself:

"Well, old Joe, you've bagged all sort o' game in this 'ere forest, and trapped 'most everything a-goin', but you ain't never had such a rare bit o' luck as this. No wonder I stood there on the edge of the timber-land, listening to I did n't know what! Reckon here's a couple o' skins now'll be putty popular at *one* market at any rate,— fetch 'most any price you could name. But I'll let 'em go cheap; all the pay I want for these 'ere critters is jest to see the antics of them poor frightened — Hello! there's a light! What, ahoy! Neighbor, hello! hello!"

"Got 'em both!" he shouted, as three figures, two men and a woman, came in sight through the starlight. "All right — got 'em both!"

The children are awake now. What sobs, what laughter, what broken words of gratitude and joy, fall upon the midnight air! Little Nat utters only a faint "Hello, Papa! hello, Mama!" as he slides from Trapper Joe's strong hold into his mother's outstretched arms.

Mother, Father, Trapper Joe, and the neighbor seem all to be talking at once — and Winnie, wondering and thrilled with strange happiness, is saying to herself: "I knew God would show us the way home!"

THE BRIGHTON CATS

MAY AND MABEL.

MABEL AND MAY, the twins, were very fond of cats. From the time when they first toddled about the house and garden, they had a pet kitten that was their special pride and joy. Strange to say, under these circumstances, this kitten had a very comfortable though active existence, and seemed to think that, instead of the twins owning it, it owned the twins.

Well, one happy day when May and Mabel were eight years old, their Uncle Jack came home from a long visit — in fact, as Mabel said, he had been away from them "a whole half-year." He always had lived on Long Island, but now he had been to Europe, and that, the twins insisted, "made a great difference." He had seen the bears at Berne; the poll-parrots at Havre; the lions and tigers at Hamburg; the monstrous birds and all the wonderful things in the Jardin des Plantes in Paris; and the fishes and sea-marvels in the London Aquarium. But best of all, to the twins, he had seen the amazing and delightful Brighton cats — those highly intelligent and dramatic creatures that, at one time, were celebrated throughout Great Britain.

12   177

It was on a winter evening, after their early supper, that the twins first heard about the Brighton cats. Uncle Jack, bowing elegantly, asked them to "step into the library, please."

When they were cozily seated by the big table, he observed: "I believe you two like cats and kittens best of all your animal friends."

"Oh, yes! indeed we do!" exclaimed the twins.

At this, Uncle Jack ran his hand deep down into the inner breast-pocket of his coat, and held it there mysteriously, while the twins waited eagerly to see what new surprise was coming. Slowly he drew forth a small packet of pictures, carefully laying them before him, backs up.

"Oh!" said Mabel.

"Oh!" said May.

"Just so," remarked Uncle Jack. "We understand one another perfectly." And, somehow, he contrived by his tone and manner to let them know that he highly approved of their patient politeness, and that he would now proceed.

And this is the story he told them — true from beginning to end. And the pictures of the Brighton cats, shown in these pages, are carefully copied from the very photographs that Uncle Jack took from his pocket that evening.

DID ever you hear of the Brighton cats? No? Well, that is strange, for they are very famous fellows, I assure you. Brighton is in England, you must know. They are trained cats, and they are not only very good actors, but, what is more pleasant still, they seem to enjoy their own

performances very much. Their master loves them dearly,
and every day they jump up on his shoulders, and, rubbing
their soft cheeks against his beard, purr gently, as if to
say, "Ah, master dear, if it were not for you, how stupid

PUMPKINS PAINTS.

we should be! You have taught us everything." Then
the master laughs and strokes them, before he sets them
at work. Then he says:

"Pussies, attention!"

Down they jump, their eyes flashing, their ears twitching and eager, their very tails saying —"Aye, aye, sir."

"Pimpkins, to work!"

Pimpkins is a painter; that is, he has learned to hold a palette and mahlstick in one paw, and a brush in the other, which you'll admit is doing very well for a cat. With his master's help, he is soon in readiness, perched upon a stool and painting away for dear life on the canvas before him. There is always a very queer-looking picture on the easel unfinished, and pussy daubs away at it when

A GAME OF CHESS.

visitors are by; but when asked whether he did it all or not, he keeps very still, and so does his master.

Meantime the two other pussies, whom we must know as Tib and Miss Moffit, obeying a signal from the master, seat themselves at a table, and begin a lively game at chess. The chessmen stand in proper order at first, and both pussies look at them with an air of unconcern. Soon

Tib moves his man. Then Miss Moffit moves hers. On comes Tib again, this time moving two men at once. Instantly Moffit moves three. The game now grows serious. Moffit's men press so thickly on Tib's that suddenly he gives all of them a shove, and Miss Moffit is check-mated! *Then* Tib is grand. Leaning his elbows on the table, and

MISS MOFFIT HANGS THE CLOTHES TO DRY.

tipping his head sideways, he looks severely at Moffit until she fairly glares.

After this all the pussies are, perhaps, requested to wash for their master. And they do it, too, in fine style, though, when they are through, Tib and Pimpkins generally squabble for a bath in the tub, or pretend to do so. The fact is, they hate soapy water; but being great actors, they scorn to show their real feelings while performing. Meanwhile Miss Moffit takes the clothes they

12*

are supposed to have washed, and demurely hangs them on the line to dry.

After work comes play. Miss Moffit and Pimpkins have a little waltz, and Tib slides down the balusters. Sometimes Tib amuses himself by drawing the cork from

MISS MOFFIT AND PIMPKINS WALTZ.

his master's ale-bottle. And then if the foaming ale happens to be unusually lively, it makes a leap for Tib, and Tib rubs his nose with his paws for five minutes afterward.

Are they ever naughty? Yes, indeed. But even then their good master is gentle with them. He never whips them, but simply looks injured, and orders them to " do

TIB ACTS AS BUTLER.

penance." Poor Tib and Moffit,—for they generally are the naughty ones,—how they hate this! But they never think of such a thing as escaping the punishment. No, indeed; they jump upon a chair at once, and, shutting their eyes, stand as you see them in the picture, two images of misery, until their master says they may get down.

What else can they do? Why, ever so many bright things, I suppose, though I have told you of all that comes to my mind at present. Ah, yes, they bowed; yes, all three stood in a line and bowed gravely whenever the pleased audience applauded very warmly. Sometimes, too, they would place their right paws upon their hearts as they bowed; but this was an uncertain part of the performance, and their master pretended not to notice when they failed.

One day an old woman from the country, after intently

watching these talented cats,— painting, chess-playing and all that,— shook her head solemnly. " I dunno as it's right," she said; " it 's onnatural—cuttin' about and actin' like Christians as they do."

Tib stood on his hind legs at this, and Miss Moffit shook paws with Pimpkins — as well she might.

So ended Uncle Jack's true story. While telling it he had always, at the right moment, presented May and Mabel with the fitting photograph so that they might see exactly how these Brighton cats appeared in each scene.

DOING PENANCE.

WORTH YOUR WEIGHT IN GOLD

(A TALK WITH GIRLS)

"YOU 'S JES' WUF YO' WEIGHT IN GOLE,' SHE SAY TO OLE PATSY, ONE EBENIN' IN MY KITCHUM."

WORTH YOUR WEIGHT IN GOLD

A STORY FROM LIFE

" YES, Miss Mamie, dat 's jes' what de missus sed to me. 'Aunt Patsy,' ses she, 'you 's jes' wuf yo' weight in gole.' An' so I wuz, Miss Mamie; I know'd it. Poor weak ole cull'd pusson as I is, I know'd she war tellin' d' exac' trufe. De Lord knows 't ain't no vain-gloruf'cation fur ole Patsy t' say dem words. I don' take no pus'nal credit 'bout it, Miss Mamie. Cookin' takes practice, but it 's got to come fus' by natur'. De ang'l Gabr'el hisse'f could n't make a cook out o' some folks. It 's got to be born inter yer like. I 'se mighty 'umble and fearful ub myse'f 'bout some t'ings, but not 'bout cookin'. *Dat* I un'stan'; an' dat 's what made me wuf my weight in gole. Missus did n' hab no sort troubl' 'bout nothin' af'er once dis chile come. 'You 's jes' wuf yo' weight in gole,' she say to ole Patsy one ebenin' in my kitchum, when I was a-gettin' de supper ready for de fam'ly. She *say* so. Ain't no use talkin' 'bout it—dem 's her 'cise words ter prove it.

" Well, de work wuz mighty heavy in dat house. Stacks o' comp'ny, and massa war one ob dem perwiders dat don' hab no sort o' notion how many pots kin go onto de stobe,

and seem t' t'ink de oben was 'mos' big as de barn.   Many's
de time I got so tired seem'd to me 's if I 'd drop; but
af'er missus sed *dat*, I did n' mind nuffin'.   'Patsy,' sez İ,
when I seed myse'f gettin' done up, 'yer goo' f' nuffin' lazy
nigger, wha' 's matter wid yer?   Don' yer know yer 's wuf
yo' weight in gole?'—and dat nd fotch me squar' up.
Many 's de time I 'se sed dem words to myse'f sence dat
day, but wid dis diff'ence: Missus, dear soul! she done
gone to Ab'am's bosom four year 'go; an' ole Patsy eber
sence 's been mos' too fur on wid dis ere cough to be much
'count to white folks—and so I keep sayin' to myse'f,
'Yer *wuz* wuf yer weight in gole.   Don' you nebber forgit
dat.' "

And, all this time, the brightly kerchiefed and check-
aproned speaker was going on briskly with her work, while
I sat looking at her with an amused smile?

Not a bit of it.   She was helpless in bed, dying of con-
sumption, and my heart was full of reverence as I stood
gently fanning her.   She was talking beyond her strength,
but I knew it was useless to check her while her thoughts
were with this treasured saying of her "missus."   Presently
she sank into a doze.   I stood there, afraid to move lest I
should wake her.

In a few moments she opened her eyes.

"Bress yer heart, Miss Mamie, don' stan' dere no longer.   Ole Patsy don' want ter be nussed like she war a
queen."

Her eyes were so bright and her tones so cheerful that I
thought she was going to laugh; but, instead, she said
softly:

"'T ain't fur much longer, Honey; de Lord 'll soon sen' his char'ot an' take me to glory."

She ceased speaking. I knew by her face, though not a sound could be heard, that she was singing under her breath one of the dear old negro hymns that we had been used to hearing when she was up and at work; and then she fell into another doze.

Two weeks from that day the chariot came.

HAPPY old Aunt Patsy! Even with the memory of her illness and suffering fresh in mind, I always think of her as "happy old Aunt Patsy," for had she not been worth her weight in gold? The dear old woman always laid great stress not at being prized at her weight in gold, but in being really *wuf it*. That was the point. And the best of it was that her precious weight being mainly in her value as a good servant, it increased just so much in proportion as she excelled. Simple-hearted creature though she was, she would have scorned the idea of weight, in this connection, being a matter of mere flesh and bones. No, it was Patsy the cook who was weighed in the balance.

It seems to me now that if I had seen Aunt Patsy when I was a little girl, and heard her tell her story, it would have been a great help. It would have taught me, in one easy lesson, that to be worth your weight in gold is a great advantage, and that the best way of becoming worth your weight in gold is to learn to do some one thing thoroughly well. Aunt Patsy could cook. That is a fine thing in itself. Cooking is a good business when one has one's living to make, and a valuable accomplishment when one has a living ready-made. Every one of us girls, little and big, young and old, should know something about it, and should seize all good opportunities to improve in the art. But I am not going to ask you to learn to cook; that is, not now; especially if it is not "born into you." I only throw out as a friendly suggestion the idea that every girl should make it an object, as Aunt Patsy did, to learn to do one thing well at a time. If, as a start, she selects some style of housework, so much the better. Let it be sweeping and dusting; let it be bed-making; let it be clear-starching, silver-cleaning or cutting and sewing, or even one branch of cookery, such as bread-making, or that rare art, potato-boiling. Let her aim at real excellence in any one of these, taking the most exact pains, looking out day by day for ways of improvement, aiming to excel herself at each effort, until, at last, "Jenny did it" (or whatever her fortunate name may be) shall stand as a guarantee for excellence in this or that special department. Let Jenny's butter, or Jenny's bread, be the best her father and mother ever tasted; or let them feel that no one else can so brighten the silver, or the tins, or furniture; that it is sure to be all right if Jenny but sweeps the halls and stairs, or Jenny but makes the pudding,—"It's her specialty, you know,"—and you will see, if you are Jenny, what satisfaction there is in it.

Then, when one style of work is mastered, another can be taken up and made a study; and so on, till you are worth your weight in gold to your family. Mind, I do not mean to say that while these special endeavors are going

on you are to do all other work carelessly and without interest. Not so, of course. I mean only that one branch at
a time shall receive most care and attention till it is mastered to the utmost of your ability. Nor do I mean that
you are to spend all of your young life in housework. An
average of half an hour a day devoted to such work, or
even less, all through one's girlhood, will in many cases be
all that is necessary or desirable. But certainly a girl is
to be pitied who never is taught to sew, nor given an opportunity to learn practically the rudiments of housewifery.
I hope none of you who read this are so unfortunate.

There are other fields of effort which you may cultivate.
Sewing or music, reading, fancy-work, drawing, certain
school-studies, gardening — whichever of them seems most
attractive to you — will serve as a starting-point. I have
dwelt principally upon the art of cooking, because Aunt
Patsy set me talking; but there are many fair paths opening in every direction. Take the one nearest by, whether
it lead to the kitchen, the parlor, the library, or out of
doors. But be sure to be thorough as you go along. Don't
shimble-shamble through everything, and then wonder
that those who love you best are not quite satisfied with
your progress —that you do not really add to any one's
comfort or interest; in short, that you are not your worth
in gold.

"I love books best, but can I be a help to anybody at
home if I sit and read all day?" you may ask.

And I answer, you cannot. If you read too much, you
are not reading well. If you read too steadily, you are not

reading well. And if you read books that do not make you more intelligent, more sunny, more charitable and high-minded than you otherwise would be, you are reading very badly indeed. If you sit reading for hours, selfishly neglecting some duty, and filling your mind with false ideas of life, and arousing thoughts that in your secret heart you know are not good for you, you are doing an injury, not only to yourself, but to others with whom you hence-forth may be brought in contact.

But if at seasonable times, and after proper intervals of play or bodily exercise, you read in an inquiring, sincere way books that entertain or instruct the best part of you (we all soon find out what that best part of our nature is), and that have been selected under guidance of some one competent to help you, then you *are* doing good to others as well as to yourself, by reading. You hardly can go up or down stairs when in the mood such reading engenders with-out doing somebody good. If it is only the cat on the land-ing, she 'll get the benefit of it somehow. A sunny, healthy mind sheds beams of light unconsciously; and then there are the cheery word, the pleasant smile, the ready spirit of fun, the thoughtful question or answer, the entertaining bubbles of talk that rise to the surface of a mind set sparkling by good books worthily read. You will soon find the value of it all,— or some one else will.

It is not so much what good thing we do, though that is of great consequence, but how well we do it that deter-mines our success. A pragmatic, conceited manner, or a too selfish eagerness, will spoil any pursuit. There is such a thing, you must know, as being unpleasantly pleasant, meanly generous, incompetently competent, or even wickedly pious. If you will think a moment, you will see that it must be so.

For instance, a gift that really is of help to one needing it may be given in the spirit of display or of rivalry with some other giver. This is not true generosity. A merely surface quality, however effective to outsiders, cannot be the same as a quality which is so true, so deep and genuine, so in the grain from use and steady growth, that it has become a part of one's own soul.

Doubtless circumstances make the paths of improvement easy for some and difficult for others — but a life that is easy at the start is not necessarily a fortunate life. Hindering things sometimes are the stepping-stones to prosperity and peace. I know to-day noble women whose lives are the fitting flower of a beautiful, happy, industrious girlhood — women who did not spend their early, most impressive years solely for enjoyment's sake, with a vague sense of something far ahead, called life, which had very little to do with their present plans and pleasures — even with their studies and occupations.

Some persons, if once started on a road, will be so confident of their way that they 'll forget to make the proper turnings ; and there *are* persons who, in their tremendous efforts for usefulness or self-improvement, make all around them uneasy and uncomfortable. That is over-zeal. Such persons are not worth their weight in gold to anybody. Then we have the self-satisfied kind, the worst of all, perhaps. Self-satisfaction is a wall that, builded by a girl's own vanity, shuts her in completely. She cannot get outside of

13

it herself, and no one cares to scale it in order to get at her. A state of entire self-satisfaction is the loneliest thing on earth. Self-approbation is another matter. It is worth trying for because it is, in itself, good. But we must build steps with it, not walls.

That is what Aunt Patsy did. She cooked better and better every day. She worked hard for self-approbation, and slowly made it her stairway. Steadily she mounted, always humble and fearful of herself, but always hearing her mistress's words, "worth your weight in gold"; and when at last she stood on the top of the little flight, she felt sure the Lord was pleased that Old Patsy had been of use to somebody.

To-day, in the soft twilight,— a golden haze slowly hiding the hilltops, gentle memories gathering within my soul,— I can hear the echo of Aunt Patsy's sweet refrain:

> "Swing low, sweet chariot,
> Comin' for to carry me home."

BIANCA AND BEPPO

"'HARK!' SAID BEPPO; 'WHAT IS THAT?'"

BIANCA and Beppo were two little Italian children. Their father was a Duke, and they lived years and years ago when many of the Dukes of Italy were at war with one another. Young as they were, Bianca and Beppo were used to the sight of grim cavalcades of armed men and mail-clad warriors.

It was a beautiful castle, adorned with fine pictures, tapestries, and statues. Gay flowers bloomed at many a window; and the colors on the walls and floors were so cunningly mingled that they were known to be there only by a sense of brightness that filled the great rooms. There were singing birds, too, that sang just as our birds sing to-day. But pictures, or flowers, or birds, were not half so bright, blooming, and merry as Beppo and Bianca. Their father often said that the very armor in his halls tingled with their childish laughter.

One day their mother, with an armed escort composed of the most trusty of the duke's retainers, went away on a visit to her father, a fierce old Baron, whose castle was many miles distant in the heart of the Apennines. That very night trouble came to the home where these children dwelt. In their little carved and gilded beds, side by side, they were wakened by a sudden commotion, as if men were scuffling below; and after that they could not go to sleep again, because the castle was so very, very still. For a long time they lay trembling and silent; at last Beppo said:

"Bianca, wait thou here. I will go down and rouse our father. Perhaps he is still asleep. What if evil work has been done?"

"Nay, Beppo," said Bianca, shuddering, "our men have been fighting, and it may be their swords are drawn yet. Do not go among them. Thou knowest how the people of the wicked Duke Faustino fell upon young Martigni one night when they were drunken, and would have killed him had not help come. Martigni is taller by a head than thou art."

"Aye, but the duke's men are not overloyal to his house; besides," said Beppo, proudly, "I could handle a sword myself, if need be."

"Take me with thee," said Bianca.

So the two children rose softly, and hastily putting on their clothes, stole down the dark stone stairway together. A ray of moonlight, coming through a high, narrow window overhead, made them start, but when they reached their father's chamber and found the door wide open, the bed empty, disordered, and signs of violence in the moonlighted room, they clung to each other in dread and terror.

"What ho! without there!" cried Beppo, finding voice at last.

There was no answer.

Bianca, hardly knowing what she did, ran screaming from the chamber, out into the long dark hall, and on through the great oaken door, which, to her surprise, was wide open. Finally, she stood irresolute upon the marble terrace.

Beppo followed her. On his way he saw one of the duke's chief attendants lying very still.

" Fesco ! Fesco ! are you hurt ?" called Beppo, again and again.

But Fesco did not answer; and with a shudder, the boy bounded past him and joined Bianca on the terrace.

Down the long broad walk, past the beautiful garden, and out through the open gateway they flew together, two scantily-clad little children, chilly with fear on that warm, bright night, and trembling at every sound. Oh, if their father were but with them !

The forest was near by — gloomy and grim now in its shadows, but safer, at any rate, than the open highway They would hide there, they thought, till morning.

But night was nearly over; very soon the faint pink streaks that lit the edge of the sky spread and grew brighter and brighter. The children sat on a mossy mound for a while and with tearful eyes watched the growing light. Then Bianca remembered some fruit that she had stowed the day before in the satchel hanging from her girdle. She put it into Beppo's cap, and begged him to eat.

" I cannot," said Beppo. " Hark ! What is that ?"

They listened. It was a faint sound as of some one moaning.

" Oh ! oh !" sobbed Bianca, " what can it be ?"

But when Beppo rose and bravely ran in the direction of the sound, she followed him, and peered as sharply as he into every bush. Suddenly Beppo sprang forward with a joyful cry.

He had seen his father.

In an instant the two children were bending over him, eagerly trying to catch his indistinct words.

"I have been wounded, my little ones," he said, slowly; "can you bring me water?"

They did not wait to wring their hands and cry. Beppo, forgetting his fears,—forgetting everything but that his father needed help,—flew to his home.

At the portal, whom should he see but Fesco, standing in the doorway, staring wildly about him.

The water was soon obtained, though it might have been brought sooner, if Beppo, in his excitement, had not forgotten the little stream near the great sycamore. And Beppo and Fesco ran to the forest together.

When they reached the spot where the duke lay, Bianca, under her father's directions, was doing all she could to bathe his wound; her little face was very pale, but she looked up with a bright smile as Beppo approached.

"Father says he will get well, Beppo, but we are not to move him from this soft bed, he says. See, I have heaped leaves under his head, and I have brought water in my hands from the brook."

It is a long, long story, if you hear every word of it; but you will be glad to get quickly to its ending. Beppo was right; there had been evil work. The duke had been dragged from the castle and stabbed. His guilty, frightened assassins, thinking him dead, had thrown him into the forest. All of the duke's servants, excepting Fesco, had either been badly wounded or had fled in terror at the first alarm. He had been drugged, and had slept so heavily, that, but for the fresh night-air blowing in upon him, he might never have wakened.

Fesco now tried to persuade his wounded master to be taken back to his own chamber, but the duke would not consent. He lay concealed in the forest for a week, and every day his children tended him faithfully. They brought him cooling drinks and fruits, and fanned him when the breezes were low; and as he grew better they sang sweet little songs to him, and carried messages back and forth between the duke and Fesco.

Meantime the frightened servants had returned; but Fesco knew he could not trust them with his secret. Only Mino, the old nurse, was told that the duke was alive, and that the children must be allowed to go to him; but Fesco threatened her with such terrible things if she breathed a word about it, that she was only too glad to pretend to mourn for her master with a grief that seemed as genuine as that of the other servants. Through the faithful Fesco, the duke contrived to send word to his wife, bidding her stay in safe quarters for a while, until he should be able to join her. The two children, busy as bees, and thoughtful night and day for their dear patient hidden in the forest, were secretly happy as children could be — despite the somber black in which they had been clothed by old Mino. It was Bianca's delight to gather flowers in the coolest places and heap them up under her father's head;

and Beppo was proud to stand guard, sword in hand, ready to fight off any enemy that might approach.

But no enemy came; only the good friends health and strength. And one dark night the duke and the children, cleverly disguised by Fesco, were driven away in an old wagon for miles and miles, until at last they came to a shepherd's cottage, where the duchess was waiting for them; and a happier meeting than theirs never took place on earth.

After that, Beppo's father and mother went to live, for a while, in Germany, taking their children with them, while Fesco stayed at home to look after his master's possessions. But one fine day, the warfare came to an end, as all things do soon or late; and, his troubles over, the duke was free again. He and his family were able to go back and live in their castle peacefully and happily; and once more the armor on the old walls tingled with the merry laughter of Bianca and Beppo.

A LAW THAT COULD NOT BE BROKEN

"'OLD MR. FEATHER-BED! ALL YOU 'VE GOT TO DO IS TO CATCH IT.'"

A LAW THAT COULD NOT BE BROKEN

A YOUNG LAWYER'S STORY

ONE evening I was reading aloud to my wife,— not one of my "never-ending law books," as she called them, but something, to my mind, much heavier. My wife had a strange fancy for primary scientific reading, and I as a wise husband humored her taste whenever I could. So this time the book chanced to be one called Arnott's "Physics or Natural Philosophy." Suddenly, in the very middle of a sentence, I laughed aloud.

Now, Arnott's "Physics" is by no means a droll book. I am quite sure there is not a joke in it, from cover to cover. So, when I laughed, my wife looked up in great surprise, for, naturally, my reading had put the dear little lady in a decidedly thoughtful mood.

"What is it, Rob?" she asked, smiling in spite of herself when she met my broad grin.

"This part here, about the center of gravity and its always taking the proper place," answered I, tapping the page with my fingers, "made me think of something."

"Did it?" she said with solemn surprise.

As the precious girl—please don't mind my speaking in this way of my little wife, for, the fact is, we have been married but two years, and she is just twenty to my twenty-five,—as the precious girl evidently did not expect an answer to her question, I took up the book again and read:

"By attending to the center of gravity of the bodies around us on the earth, we are enabled to explain why, from the influence of gravity, some of them are stable, or firmly fixed, others tottering, others falling. * * * The line of a plummet hanging from the center of gravity is called the line of direction of the center, or that in which it tends naturally to descend to the earth.

"You remember, Lily," said I, interrupting myself, "the law we read in Gale yesterday:

"While the line of direction falls *within the base* upon which the body stands, the body cannot upset; but if the line fall beyond the base, the body will tumble."

Then, taking a pencil and note-book from my pocket, I made a picture of a coach tilted by a great stone in such a way that a perpendicular line drawn from its center of gravity fell *beyond the base* of the coach, that is, outside of the point where its wheels touched the ground, and she saw at a glance, with a little womanly shiver, that the coach must upset.

"Oh, yes, I understand it now, perfectly," she exclaimed, quite pleased.

So I read on, as Dr. Arnott proceeded to tell us how to find the center of gravity of any object, and to explain in a very clear and delightful way the principle shown in rolling balls, leaning towers, and unsafe chimneys; in the graceful positions of skaters; in tumbling dolls and the movements of various toys,—

" Rob ! " exclaimed my wife.

" No, dear," said I, listening a moment and thinking that she had fancied she heard the baby cry.

" Rob ! " she exclaimed again, " what were you laughing about ? "

" When ? " said I.

" Why, a moment ago."

" Oh," I said, " did n't I ever tell you, my dear ? It was such a capital illustration of the laws we have just been studying, though I did n't know it at the time."

" Well ? " said she.

She drew her chair close to mine, with a comical look of curiosity on her face, and I began in a dramatic voice:

" 'T is now about fifteen years since a small boy, full of mischief by nature, but very cautious by education, found himself alone in the upper part of a fine city mansion. His mother was out. The servants were in the kitchen, and this small boy felt that, perhaps, never again would he have such a grand chance to be up to—something, he hardly knew what."

" Was it you, Rob ? "

" It was," said I. " Well, as the boys say, I cast about for some time, not able to settle on a plan. Many delight-ful projects entered my head, but they were all more or less connected with danger. There was the roof, as steep and as slanting as heart of boy could wish ; but I had been made so thoroughly to understand that to tumble from it would be to break every bone in my body, to say nothing of being ' killed stone dead,' that I gave up my half-formed plan at once. Then there was the window. It would be fun to let myself down from it by tying a stout rope to the bed-post, and so sliding to the ground. But the rope might break, or I might not be able to hold on — and the wild thought was abandoned in a flash. Suddenly an idea came to me:

"There was a beautiful porcelain vase on the top of father's bookcase, high out of reach. Often had I longed to see it near by, or perhaps to take it into my own hands, but always I had been met by a harrowing array of reasons why my wish could not be gratified. In the first place the vase was precious — secondly, it was fragile — thirdly, it was expensive — fourthly, it had been firmly perched upon the top of that solid bookcase so that it might be 'safely out of harm's way'—fifthly, there was no sense in my desiring a nearer view of it, a sharp-eyed little fellow like me — sixthly, they had no time to bother with such nonsense — seventhly, they would n't, and so on, till, in the course of time, I had been given twenty good reasons, more or less, why that vase should n't, could n't, and must n't be disturbed. These, of course, were soon twisted by my perverse but most lovable self into twenty or less good reasons why I should, could, and must hold that vase in my own hands and enjoy a good, long, lingering look at it. Now was my opportunity. Why not? 'There was no one nigh to hinder.' But —

"*What if I should break it!*

"A happy thought came. Nothing could harm it if I only could put a feather-bed between it and destruction. I knew where there was a fine fat one. Glorious! now I could manage to pull the vase down from its perch as easy as a wink, and without breaking it!"

"You little goose! — *then*, not now," added Mrs. Robert, hastily.

"Goose or not, I tried it," said I. "It was nearly time for mother to return. There was not a moment to be lost, and I had to make important preparations.

"The bed was made up in fine style, with its great ruffled pillow fixings and its silken spread all tucked in as if it were never to come out again. But I hauled off the covers, and with many a tug and pull brought the feather-bed to the floor. Then I dragged it to the book-case. The next thing was to fetch a step-ladder from the garret — no easy job for a ten-year-old. This done, it was evident I should need some sort of a stick with which I could tenderly start the vase. Father's umbrella with its crooked handle was just the thing.

"'Good!' said I to myself. 'Won't it be larks to knock down the vase and never hurt it a bit! Good for you, too, Old Mr. Feather-Bed! All you 've got to do is to catch it.'

"With this, seizing the umbrella after the manner of the boy and flag in 'Excelsior,' and hastily adjusting the ladder, I mounted to the top and—"

"O Rob!" cried Mrs. Robert, laughing. "I remember hearing all about it! Yes, just as well as if it were yesterday. Your mother had been to our house, and *my* mother had gone home with her. They went right

14

up-stairs, and just as they opened the door they heard such a crash, and there were you and the ladder on the floor! No, the ladder was on the feather-bed, mama said, and you were on the floor. You must have pitched over backward, Rob, just as the ladder slipped from under you."

"Very likely," said I.

"Well, I declare! That *was* a caper! What a funny little wisp of a boy you were! And to think of our actually being married thirteen years afterward! But what about the vase?"

"Oh, that was safe enough, you may be sure, for the umbrella had n't time to touch it."

"Rob," said Mrs. Robert, "if you had opened that ladder a little wider, or taken a plummet up with you and been careful to have the line of direction from the center of gravity fall within the base of the ladder, all would have been well, would n't it, my—"

Just then little Rob was heard in the next room screaming like a good fellow. Off ran Mrs. Robert. I was left alone to ponder over the laws of gravitation.

A GARRET ADVENTURE

"AT LAST THE POND BEGAN TO SHOW, IN EARNEST."

A GARRET ADVENTURE

"Snow! snow! snow!"

So it did! But Ned Brant need not have been so cross about it. He seemed to think, as he said the words, that, of all unfortunate, ill-used fellows, he was the most to be pitied; and, of all hateful, malignant things, those soft, white, downy specks, flitting past the window, were hatefulest and most malignant.

"Christmas week, too, and new skates! new skates and no skating!" said Ned, bitterly.

So it was; and perhaps the snow ought to have been ashamed of itself; but it did n't seem to be.

At this moment a great clattering was heard at the back door.

"They 've come! after all," cried Ned, rushing out of the room and down the stairs, all his wretchedness gone in an instant.

His two sisters were at the door before him, and the three opened it together.

"Oh, oh, howdy-do? we were afraid you would n't come!" said some voices, and "Hello! where 's your

14*   213

scraper?" "Pooh! we were n't going to mind such a little snow as this," cried others, all in a chorus.

Six visitors! Think of that. Two lived next door on one side, two lived next door on the other side, and two lived right across the way. The first pair were Wilbur and Rob; the second pair were Herbert and Dickie; the third pair were Jamie and Tommy. Wilbur had on an overcoat and a muffler, for he had a weak chest. Rob had a tippet tied over his cap, for he was subject to ear-ache. Herbert had a cap and a gray overcoat; Dickie had a cap and no overcoat; Jamie wore a Scotch suit; and Tommy wore a short bob-jacket and long trousers. I tell you this so that you may know how they appeared. As for their faces, they were so rosy and bright that they all looked alike when the door opened. All the visitors were boys, as any one would have known who heard the tramping as the party went up-stairs.

Yes, up-stairs they went, nine of them, talking every step of the way. The home children, Ned, Ruth and Dot, almost always took any visitor that came, right to their mother's room either to introduce them, or, at any rate, to give them the benefit of her hearty "How do you do, my dears?" But this time they went straight past her door, up, up, to the very garret.

"Ned," his mother had said in the morning, "if the children come this afternoon to help you keep the holidays, either play in the yard or up in the garret, for I shall be quite busy. Have all the fun you can, but be sure not to break anything and not to take cold."

You may wonder why Mrs. Brant did not say: "Be

sure not to be naughty." But she would almost as soon have said : " Be sure not to cut off your heads," as to have said *that*. She knew her children too well to think they did not wish to be good. As for telling them "not to take cold," that only meant they must be sure to dress warmly if they played out of doors. The garret was never very chilly, because the heat from the furnace always crept up there whenever it had a chance.

It was a lovely old garret, light, yet mysterious, with plenty of stored-away things in it to make it interesting, and a great cleared space to play in. Just now it was even more delightful than usual, for in one corner of it was a very big heap of "potter's clay."

" Oh, what 's that ? " cried the visitors, the moment they reached the garret door.

"That 's potter's clay," said Ruth. " It 's splendid for lots of things. Father 's going to make some kind of what-you-call-'ems out of it."

Thereupon the six visitors all stood in a row and gazed at the heap. It was gray, dusty and lumpy, and looked something like faded-out garden soil.

" *What 's* he going to make ? " said Tommy.

" I don't know, exactly," said Ruth, " it only came yesterday."

" Was it a Christmas present to your papa ? " asked little Dickie, innocently.

" No, indeed," replied Ned, with lofty scorn. "He had slippers. What 'd your father get ? "

" Slippers, too," said Dickie.

" So did my papa," remarked Wilbur, laughing.

"I guess all gentlemens get 'em," said Dickie, thought-fully, "but I 'd rather have 'most anything 'sides them."

Still the children stood staring at the heap of clay.

"Let 's sit on it," said Jamie, with great daring. "I guess it 'll dust off."

A hint was enough. The heap soon was covered with children, and when they jumped up they found that Jamie was right. It "dusted off" admirably.

"Let 's make a road," cried one of the others.

"All right!" said Ned, in great glee; but he looked at Ruth, and she answered his look with, "Yes; we 'd best ask Mama."

Ned was down the garret stairs in a twinkling. Then on the next flight he stopped half-way and called: "Mother! Mother! may we play with the clay?" No answer came; so he ran on down. Mrs. Brant was very busy, fitting a dress for her mother.

"Don't come in, Ned!" she called, as Ned knocked at the door. "I 'm busy with Grandma; what do you want?"

"May we play with the clay, Mother?"

"Oh, yes, I suppose so," said the mother, pinning a plait on Grandma's shoulder; "do what you please with it, only don't throw it about and get it into one another's eyes."

"Oh, no, certainly not," answered Ned, as he rushed toward the garret stairs again, quite delighted.

But when he reached the top he found all the children with tears in their eyes.

They had already forgotten the clay; for Ruth had taken a big onion from a bunch that hung on one of the rafters. Wilbur had cut it in slices, and now every one was holding a piece to see "which could smell the onion longest without crying."

"What a pack of ninnies!" cried Ned, laughing, and all the ninnies laughed with him, except little Dot, who whined a little and wished she had not tried it.

"Have you given up the road?" asked Ned, but nobody answered him, for that old garret had so much in it to look at, so many odd nooks and corners, that before the eight pairs of eyes were dry their owners were all scudding and burrowing about like so many rabbits. What a delightful time they had! I cannot begin to tell you all the games they played, and the comical talks they had, nor how they "dressed up" in the old hats and garments they found hanging on the nails, nor how the boys made the girls scream by crying, "Look out! a rat! kill him! kill him!" and then flinging their victim across the floor in the shape of an old boot or a bit of torn fur. At last Tommy looked out of one of the little square windows, which was half covered with cobwebs. "I say, it's snowing harder than ever—there'd have been good skating by to-morrow if it hadn't snowed!"

This had the effect of making all the party serious for a moment.

"It isn't so very bad," said Ruth, who always looked on the bright side of things. "There'll be splendid snowballing."

"Who cares for snowballing!" cried little Dickie, "skatin's the best."

Everybody laughed at this, for Dickie was only six years old, and couldn't skate a stroke, not even on roller skates.

Suddenly Wilbur cried, "Oh!" and stood motionless, looking steadily at the floor. Rob flew to him like a good brother, as he was, and gave him a poke.

"What on earth 's the matter, Wilbur?"

"Nothing. Only I bet we could! Sure as I live we could!"

"Could *what?*" cried Tommy.

"Why, make a skating-pond *here*, right here, in this very garret!"

"Yes, you could," sneered Tommy, who, by the way, was the only fellow who had taken off his hat; Ruth had excused the others because the garret was not very warm.

"I tell you, I could, man. I say, Ned, let 's do it! We can have a pond here before night. You have a bath-room on the next floor, have n't you? Here are pots and pans enough for all of us."

All the eight stared at Wilbur, as if they thought his wits were leaving him, but he added eagerly:

"I tell you, it will be grand. We 'll have as big a circle as we can get here in the middle of the garret, and make a bank out of that clay, after we 've moistened it so it will stick together. Clay holds water perfectly. Then we 'll fill up the circle with water."

Their eyes danced at this, but Tommy chilled their ardor with a sarcastic—

"Ho! skate on water! ho!"

"We 'll open the scuttle and the windows, and let the pond freeze overnight" said Wilbur.

"Jimminy!" screamed Ned; "so we can! Come on here; we 'll have the bank in a jiffy!"

“ Hurrah !” cried the rest.

In an instant all hands were at work—all but Ruth, who looked troubled, and begged Dot to “go down and ask Mama.” She should have gone herself, for Dot was only six years old, and a very uncertain young person in the art of carrying messages.

Soon Dot, clambering down two sets of stairs, rushed into her mother’s room with, “ Mama, Ruth wants to know if we can do it ? ”

“ Do what, Dot ? (Mother, do look at that child’s cheeks —they ’re just like roses.) Do what, my pet ? ”

“ Why, play bank with the clay,” panted Dot.

“ Oh, I suppose I must,” laughed the mother. “ Tell her yes, Dot.” As the little girl ran out of the room and up the stairs, screaming, “ Yes, yes, Mama says you can do it,” Mrs. Brant said to Grandma, “ I ought to go up, I suppose. But they can’t do more than make a mess with it, and they can clear it all up to-morrow. If I were you, Mother, I ’d never let Madame Pomfret make me a gown again. I can improve this a little, but the cut was all wrong in the first place.”

“ You ’re too easy with those children, Eliza,” said Grandma, quietly, adding, as Mrs. Brant hurriedly took up her sewing again, “ but they ’re such dear little things, I don’t wonder you like to make ’em happy.”

“ Good !” cried Ned, when Dot’s happy message was de- livered. “ Mother ’s splendid. I say, we must fill up all these cracks with the clay, boys.”

“ You ’re sure Mother said we could, Dot ? ”

“ Course she did,” said Dot, decidedly. “ She laughed, too.”

Poor little Dot had no idea that she had told her mother only half of their plan. Her own head was so full of it that she thought every one else must know all about it, too. As for Ruth, she being three years older, could not help being surprised at their mother's consent to such wild fun, yet she never dreamed but that her mother had consented. It was a time of deep delight to her, for she could work as hard as any of the boys.

In a little while the bank was made. "Many hands make light work." It was a fine affair, well packed and quite regular in shape, for Wilbur had chalked a circle on the floor for them "to work by."

So before very long Ned and Tommy took two pails that were in a corner of the garret and ran to the bath-room for water. Ruth gave a pitcher to Jamie, a basin to Herbert, a tub to Wilbur, and, seizing a big earthen jar for herself, gave the word for all to follow.

It was hard work, but it passed for play, and they all played with a will. They let the water run from both of the faucets into the bath-tub, so that after a while some could fill at the faucets and others could dip as much water as they wished out of the tub.

Up and down, down and up, the laughing children went, panting and pulling, filling and pouring, bucketful, pailful, pitcherful, basinful, crockful, over and over again, till at last the pond began to show in earnest. Wilbur seized an old spade out of a broken cradle, and had as much as he could do to watch the clay bank, and mend breaks, and beat it solid with the back of the spade.

"Keep on! keep on!" shouted Ned, still leading the way,

while the rest followed. "We 'll have her full in less than
no time."

. . . .

"Eliza!" said Grandma, "do hear the tramping. What
on earth can those children be doing?"

"Oh," laughed Mrs. Brant, "they 're playing some game
or other. Betsey 'll look after them. She 's busy up-stairs,
for I hear the water running."

"It 's mighty queer," said Ned, dashing in a pailful, as
Ruth emptied her crock for the twentieth time—"mighty
queer how long it takes the thing to fill—but keep on,
fellows. Don't stop!"

In a few moments the street door opened, and in came
Mr. Brant. He went at once up to the sewing-room.

"How d' ye do, how d' ye do?" said he cheerily, kissing
Mrs. Brant and his mother. "Well, this *is* a busy party—
put up your work, my dear, and come up to the library—
I 've something to tell you and Mother. Ho! ho! here 's
baby awake. Well, we must take him up, too."

Baby shouted with delight to find himself in Papa's
arms. Mrs. Brant laid down her work, Grandma took her
crochet-basket in her hand, and they all went up to Papa's
light, pleasant library on the floor above.

"Well, my dear, what is it? Some good news, I 'm
sure," said Mrs. Brant, as Grandma nestled in her easy
chair, and Papa, setting baby on the floor with a toss and a
flourish, proceeded to place a chair for himself between
his wife and mother.

"Yes, it *is* good news, dear, I 'm happy to say," he answered, with a bright smile. "I don't know when I 've

had anything so pleasant to—Halloa, what the mischief's the matter ?"

They started up. Surely enough, something was the matter. It was raining! A shower was coming down on their heads, the ceiling was cracking, the baby screaming. Patter, patter came the water, faster and faster. What *could* it be ? Perhaps the house was on fire and the firemen already were up-stairs with their hose! The thought made Grandmother scream as she rushed to the baby's rescue. Mr. Brant dashed up the stairs, almost knocking down Dot and Rob on the way.

"What's going on up here? Quick! where does the water come from ?"

No need of asking the question. There were the pond, the startled faces of the children, the pitchers, basins and pails.

"What in the world !" cried the father, seizing a pail and scooping up as much as he could from the pond. "Here, lend a hand, all of you! Call Betsey! we must empty this as quickly as possible."

He had opened the little window by this time, had emptied the pail, and was now dipping from the pond again. The children meantime took the hint, and, opening the other window, went to work as hard as they could. Well, they emptied the pond in a quarter of the time it had taken to fill it. Mrs. Brant, Grandma and Betsey came to the rescue and did wonders with towels, sheets and everything of that sort they could lay their hands on. In her excitement, Mrs. Brant came near wiping the floor with the baby.

The worst was soon over, but it seemed the library ceiling could n't get over it in a hurry. It dripped, and dripped, and broke out in great damp blotches and cracked and whimpered as if it were alive. Fortunately, the contents of the bookcases escaped wetting, and the carpet did n't "run," as Grandma said; so it might have been worse.

But those six visitors — who shall describe their emotions! As one of them afterward said, they "were frightened to death and bursting with laughter." They all tried to hide behind one another when Mr. Brant, half angry, half amused, asked them what they would like to do next.

"Go home, sir, I guess," said Tommy.

And home they went.

BORROWING TROUBLE

"HE LAY ON THE SOFT GRASS UNDER HIS FAVORITE TREE, PONDERING
THE JESTER'S WORDS."

BORROWING TROUBLE

A FEW hundred years ago, there lived near Florence a handsome little prince and a beautiful little princess. These two children had everything that a good human heart of that day could have, excepting trouble. It seemed that this could not come to them. From the day that a careless lady of the court had remarked in Francesca's presence, "Ah, Leonardo! thou well mayst say this world has trouble enough for all," the little princess had wondered what trouble was, and why, if there was enough for all, she and her brother had none of it. Often the princess would say:

"Ferdinand, what is trouble?" And Ferdinand would reply: "Alas! Francesca, I do not know."

"Let us ask our parents to give us some," pursued Francesca; "they never refuse us anything."

But the king and queen shuddered at their request:

"No, no, dear children," they cried; "you do not know

227

what you ask.   Pray that these wicked wishes may vanish from your hearts!"

But the prince and princess were not satisfied with this answer.   They applied to the most powerful of their courtiers, and, to their great astonishment, met with a refusal, accompanied with a smile and a polite bow.   They even had recourse to the court jester.

"Ah, that trouble is a very precious thing," said the jester.   "One cannot buy it, and it is not to be had for the asking.   But one may borrow it."

"Good!" cried the delighted pair.   "We shall borrow some."

"But," added the jester, "if you borrow any, you must pay back in the same coin."

"Alas!" sighed the prince and the princess.   "How can we, if we have no trouble which belongs to us?"

"True!   There is the trouble," said the jester, as he skipped away.

"What did he mean by those words?" said the prince, nearly out of patience; "but we need not concern ourselves about what he says—he is only a fool!"

Still the prince did concern himself about it, and he lay long on the soft grass under his favorite tree that day, pondering the jester's words.

The princess sought Master Cap-and-Bells again, but the interview ended sadly; for her little highness turned away despairingly, and the jester looked sorely puzzled. "What stupidity," he muttered to himself, "for the whole court to be compelled to keep this royal youth and maiden in ignorance of such a fact as trouble—the common lot of

"THE INTERVIEW ENDED SADLY."

all!" But he flourished his bauble and jingled his bells as he danced off—for was he not the court jester?

Next, in despair, the brother and sister went in search of their faithful nurse.

"Dear Catherine," said they, "we have never had any trouble. The contessa told my lord Leonardo that there was enough in this world for all. Have you had yours?"

"Oh, yes, my darlings; I have always had more trouble than I want," wailed the old woman, shaking her head.

"Oh, oh! Give us some! Give us some, good Catherine!" eagerly exclaimed the prince and princess.

But Catherine lifted her hands in horror, and tottered away, mumbling her prayers.

15*

Then the prince and princess wandered into the garden, and sat down upon a mossy seat.

"Nobody will give us what we have asked for," said Francesca. "It is very cruel."

"Yes, very cruel," replied Ferdinand, with a sigh.

"Our parents never refused us before," resumed Francesca.

"Never!" echoed Ferdinand.

"Nor the courtiers," added Francesca.

"Nor the courtiers," echoed Ferdinand.

"Nor our dear old nurse," said Francesca, with a strange feeling in her eyes.

"Nor our dear nurse."

"It is ingratitude!"

"Very great ingratitude!"

"It is cruelty!" finished Francesca, with sobs; "and my eyes are all wet! Are yours, Ferdinand?"

"No, Francesca. But there is a choking in my throat."

Just then the chief gardener came that way.

"My dear prince and princess!" he exclaimed, throwing himself on his knees before them. "You are sad! are weeping! Oh, Heaven! to think that these noble and beautiful children should have so much trouble."

"Trouble!" echoed Ferdinand and Francesca. "Is this trouble, Antonio?"

"Assuredly, I think so," said Antonio, much puzzled.

Then the prince and princess arose gaily and clapped their hands, and ran to the palace as happy as two birds. Their wish had been gratified at last.

HEAVIER THAN AIR

THE PICTURE IN THE GALLERY.

HEAVIER THAN AIR

Once upon a time, two little French children, while being led through a picture-gallery, suddenly came upon a very startling painting by the French artist Verlat. In vain their *bonne*, or nurse, tried to draw them away. They either were too much frightened, or too much amused, to stir from the spot.

"O Matilde!" they cried, still gazing at the picture, "what does it mean? What is it all about?"

"Nothing," said Matilde. "Come away. Those dreadful, ugly things will bite you. Come, Henri!"

"Ho!" retorted Henri, stoutly. "How can a picture bite? Oh! if Mama were only here to tell us how the poor monkeys got up in the air so high!"

"I know how the blackest one got there," said the other child; "the white one pulled him up with his tail."

Henri laughed at this, but after the sober manner of one who has a great deal on his mind: "No, no, Marie, he did n't go up that way. *I* think he's holding on to that fellow's tail now so that he may not fall."

233

"Oh! oh!" exclaimed Marie, with eager sympathy. "That's it! They're both going to fall in a minute. That's why they look so frightened. O Monsieur!" she added, running up to an old gentleman who stood near by, "don't you think those monkeys are going to tumble?"

The *bonne* caught her arm with an angry *"Hist!"* but the kind old gentleman turned to look at the picture with Marie.

"Yes, my little one," he answered with a smile; "in one instant more those poor fellows will be whirling down, down, to certain destruction."

"Right upon the roofs?" Marie asked, with her eyes very wide open.

"Right upon the roofs. You see the balloon is burst."

Henri nodded wisely. He began to suspect what was the matter.

"I suppose, Monsieur, the monkeys tried to go up in a balloon, and it hit against something and bursted, and —"

"Hit against *what* thing, my little man?"

Henri and Marie peered into the picture. Marie, with a questioning glance at Monsieur, pointed to the little balloon in the corner; but he shook his head. At last Henri said:

"I think it broke its own self."

"Right!" said Monsieur. "If Mademoiselle will permit, I will tell you all about it."

The *bonne* looked troubled, wondering what Madame would say when she heard that the children had been allowed to talk with a stranger. But she nodded her head, and the old gentleman seated himself on a chair that chanced to be near by, and asked the children if they had ever seen a balloon.

"Oh, yes," said Marie; "don't you remember, Henri, how we saw one on the Emperor's birthday sailing up way over the Champs de Mars? But it was n't a bit like this thing, and it had n't any monkeys in it. It was like the little one up there in the picture."

"That looks little," said the old gentleman, "because it is very far off in the air. I have been up in a balloon even higher than that."

The children stared first at Monsieur, then at the picture, and Marie asked timidly:

"With a monkey?"

"No, no," he laughed, "not with a monkey. But once I went up at night with a scientific friend, and we took a carrier-pigeon with us. We let him loose with a note tied under his wing telling his owner that we were safe and happy and more than a mile high. And, another time, two friends and myself went up in late autumn, and actually sailed into a snow-storm, high, high over the world, and with clouds both above and below us."

Marie hardly heard. She was gazing at the picture.

"Ah! I see you must be satisfied about those apes before you will listen to anything more. One cannot tell from a picture all that has been happening; but I think this: I think those two monkeys belonged to a public garden, and one day, when a balloon was going to make its ascent from there, the monkeys jumped in before any one could stop them, and loosened the cords that held the balloon down, and up it rose high in the air, amid the

"'WE TOOK A CARRIER-PIGEON WITH US.'"

shouts and screams of the spectators. At first it was all
very fine; they enjoyed their sail and crouched in the
bottom of the balloon-car, chattering to each other at a
great rate, for they had no idea of their danger. The balloon was kept up in the air by its great, big, varnished
silk bag, being full of hydrogen gas, which is about sixteen
times lighter than air—" Then Henri spoke:

"Did it float in the air something as soap-bubbles do?
because they 're so much lighter than anything else."

"Yes," said Monsieur, wondering whether it were worth
while to explain that the soap-bubble is just a bag made
of a very thin sheet of water and filled with warm breath.
"Anything that is lighter than air, if set free, will rise. But
the air grows thinner and lighter the higher one goes up
above the earth, and when a balloon gets into very thin
air, the gas within the bag, finding that it is not pressed upon
so much by the heavy air outside, begins to swell and try to
get out; and the higher it goes, the more the gas pushes,
until, at last, it bursts the bag—*then* what happens?"

"The monkeys get frightened," said Marie, gazing earn-
estly at the picture.

Henri was older and wiser; so he answered that "most
likely the balloon would all shrivel and tumble down if
the gas came out of it, just as a toy balloon would if some
one should prick it."

"Very good," assented Monsieur. "Now, in the top of
all balloons there is a valve or little door for letting out the
gas when it begins to swell, and a man seated in the balloon-car has only to pull a certain string when he wishes
to open the valve. But our monkeys knew nothing of

this. And so, after a while, their balloon burst with a terrible bang, and at once began to tumble and pitch about at such a rate that the poor fellows were bumped out of the car and had to hold on to the wreck as well as they could; for, now that the gas was out, their balloon was heavier than the air, and would have to go down."

"It's awful to be a monkey way up in a balloon, when it's all bursted," said Marie, nearly ready to cry. "Oh!" she added, suddenly turning her earnest blue eyes full upon Monsieur's face. "I do wish you had gone with them, so you could have pulled the string!"

Monsieur laughed, but the *bonne* stepped briskly forward, fearing that her little charge was growing too talkative.

"Now, children, thank the kind gentleman, and come home to Mama."

Marie took her hand willingly; but Henri had another question to ask:

"What word is that, Monsieur, printed on the balloon in the corner?"

"Montgolfier, the name of two brothers. They were the first men who ever sent a balloon up in the air. This was in the summer-time, about a hundred years ago."

"Where did they get the gas?" asked Henri, hurriedly, for the *bonne* was looking at him, with her lips pressed impatiently.

"They didn't use gas at all, my boy; they kindled a fire, and filled the bag with smoke. They thought the smoke carried up the balloon, but in reality it was the hot air, which is very much lighter than ordinary air."

BALLOONING THROUGH A SNOW-STORM.

"Oh!" said Henri, as the *bonne* took hold of his hand, "I *do* wish I could stay all day and hear more about balloons, and how often you have been up in them!"

"So do I. Ask your papa, my boy. He can tell you, I think, all about Montgolfier, and Lunardi, and Gay-Lussac, and Glaisher, and—"

"O Matilde!" cried Henri, "*do* stop your pulling! Good

day, Monsieur—I 'm very much obliged to you, Monsieur—if it was n't for Matilde, I 'd—"

And out stalked Matilde through the doorway with the children, one on each side of her; both looking back—Henri at the old gentleman, and Marie at the picture.

"O Matilde!" cried Henry indignantly, when they reached the street, "you cruel Matilde! not to let me wait and hear all about Lunardac, and Glaishac, and Montgolfy, and all the rest."

"That 's too bad!" said Marie, looking sympathetically at him across Matilde's skirts. "I 'd like to hear about 'em too—were they monkeys?"

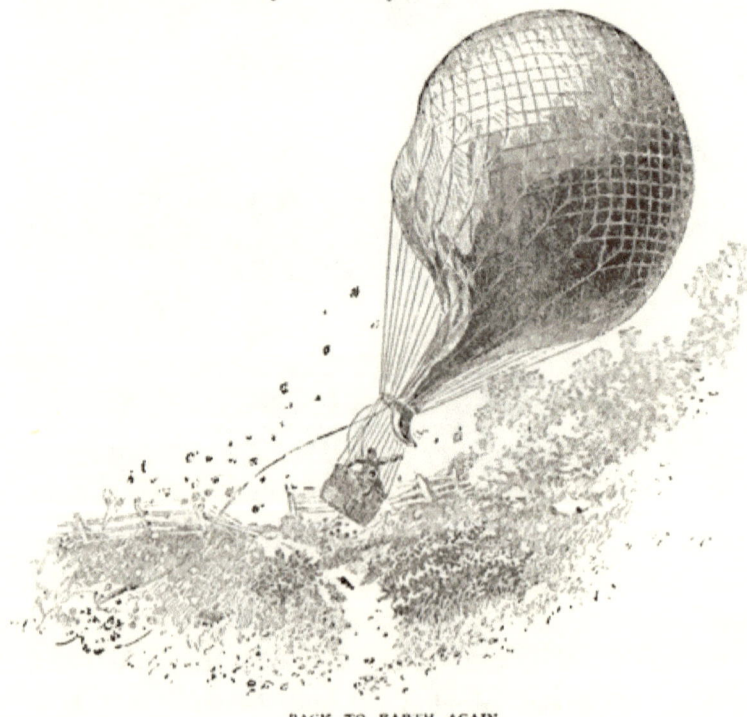

BACK TO EARTH AGAIN.

WHAT THE SNOW-MAN DID

WHAT THE SNOW-MAN DID

I⊤ was twelve years ago, and midwinter. There had
been good skating at Rockville for nearly a week; but, on
a certain cold Friday, it suddenly began to snow. The
great white flakes came down, slowly at first, then more
rapidly, until the air seemed a tumultuous mass of eider-
down. Then the ground, the fences, the trees, began to
take their share, and the whole country-side grew white.
In the city, not far off, people bemoaned the "bad walking"
that already threatened them; but country folk as promptly
looked forward to sleigh-rides and frolic.

The boys and girls of Rockville reveled in the discus-
sion of various plays for Saturday if it should keep on
snowing. Thoughts of snowballing, fort-building, coast-
ing, and all kinds of snow sport scurried through their busy
young noddles; and, as soon as they came out of school, the
boys and girls divided off into merry groups, some eagerly
chatting, some frolicking in the soft snow; while a party
of five boys dashed off toward the large, frozen pond half
a mile away. These were the shinny-boys. They had
agreed to play a game of shinny on the ice after school

the next day; but, now, as the snow threatened to stop their promised sport, they had decided not to wait, but to have their game at once.

The beautiful storm ceased as suddenly as it had begun; but that night the snow came again,—and this time to continue until morning. Then youthful existence in that region was comprised in the term, "lots of fun." The coasting-hill was crowded on that Saturday. Snow forts, hastily erected, became scenes of bold attack and desperate defense, and three hardy boys proceeded to make the biggest ball of snow ever seen in that locality; it grew and grew until it reached to their shoulders, and finally it was as much as the three could do to roll it to the edge of the precipice called in Rockville — by the young ladies "the Lovers' Leap"; and by the boys "Clifford's Jump," because a daring young fellow of that name really had jumped from it once,—and had taken a good, long rest in the hospital afterward.

Well, the mammoth ball—after the boys' ecstatic "*One, two, three! Let her go!*"—went over "Clifford's Jump" in fine style. It dashed down the steep descent, distributing itself in blocks and fragments as it went,—and was soon forgotten. The shinny-pond had yielded overnight to circumstances and become as white as its own level shores. Before dusk the forts were demolished or abandoned, and snow-day foes returned to the ways of peace.

Meantime, four fine fellows,—Hal McDougal, Charley Green, and Sydney Burton and his brother Will,—eager to enjoy their Saturday to the utmost, had assembled after early breakfast behind the McDougal cottage.

THE SHINNY BOYS HAVE THEIR GAME.

"Shall we build a fort, or a what?" asked Charley Green.

"A what," responded Sydney Burton, promptly.

"Oh, bother!" retorted Charley; "don't begin your fooling. I mean, shall we build a fort or a man? I vote for the man."

"And I 'm for a fort," put in Will.

16*

"It will be twice the fun to make a snow-man, Will," said his brother Sydney; "won't it, Charley?"

Now, Charley had a way of saying "Of course" that was worth a bushel of arguments to a boy like Will; so when he said "Of course," and Hal added scornfully, "Who wants a fort?" the thing was settled: a man it should be.

Nearly all day the boys worked. A strong clothes-pole served as a backbone around which the figure was built from the ground upward. None of them had ever made a snow-man before, and to make a large, well-shaped one was not a very easy task. Even with their determination to have him well proportioned, he turned out, as Sydney confessed, to be "rather short for his thickness"; and Will's plan of helping this trouble, by piling the snow on top of the big white head, did n't work well at all. Still he *would* insist upon holding up great balls, and shouting: "Help yourself, Syd,— pile up!"

And Sydney as resolutely shouted back:

"Don't want it. I tell you he's got twice too much forehead already."

"Fudge!" Charley would say; "take it, Syd,—make it into a hat."

"A hat would n't do any good," Sydney would insist, from the top of the barrel on which he was standing; "not a bit of good; the man himself is out of proportion. Don't you understand? I've taken a heap from the top of his noble brow already. Do you know I wish this chap were marble instead of snow? I've been thinking, ever since we began, I'd like to make a statue in earnest."

Meantime, Hal McDougal, shaping the arm, fell to thinking that if one had to get up a contrivance that would do all that a boy's arm does, what a task it would be! and, anyhow, what a wonderful thing a real arm was, with its muscles and sinews and all the little blood-vessels and jig-a-rigs. And then the rest of the machine—the heart and lungs and brain — he wished he knew all about them; he'd study it all out some day. Yes! he would begin straight off reading anatomy in the evenings — declare if he would n't. All this time he said nothing, but kept on shaping the sleeve, whistling and trying to build out something like a fist.

Charley Green, the oldest boy of them all, did n't care anything about the height of the forehead, nor did he trouble his brain by comparing this solid man of snow with the wonderful human animal. What bothered *him* was the snow itself.

" It's a gay old puzzle, anyway," he thought,—"this water. I don't wonder the Eastern tyrant had that traveler put to death (if it was the law to bowstring liars) who said that in *his* country water was sometimes like a cloud, sometimes like a feather, sometimes like solid blocks of glass. Nobody could believe it unless he saw it. And then — hang it all!— they tell you water itself is made of two gases ; and, again, that there's water in everything — even in dust. I'm going to study up on water. I'm going to find out what this sparkle in the snow means, and why melted snow tastes different from other water. I have n't cared for chemistry so far; but I'll take it up in earnest, if a fellow can really find out things by studying it."

" Halloo ! Charley," scolded Will at this point; " stop

THE BUILDING OF THE SNOW-MAN.

blowing your mittens and looking like an owl, and lend a hand here. I 'm in for breaking off this military gentleman's head and building him up higher, and clapping it on again. The shoulder-straps are easy to change."

" Fiddle for the straps," broke forth Sydney, quite out of patience. " If you heap up the shoulders, there 's your body too long, and your arms too short, and all your features too little."

" That would n't make a bit of difference," was Will's ready answer. " We could just shift the belt up, and I 'd alter the buttons in less than no time. Come on, Charley!"

" That 's just like you, Will," said Sydney. " I declare if he does n't think more of regimentals than a drum-major. I 'm goin' to scoop out the legs—no use in havin' the old general run down all in one solid piece."

" Who would n't go in for regimentals ?" retorted Will. " I never saw anything like the way all these snow-buttons have made a soldier of the old chap. Why, he was n't anything without them. The more I look at him, the more I can see no two ways about it. A man, whether he 's flesh or snow, is n't more than half a man till you make him a soldier."

Don't you see how it all ended ? Many a time has the grass grown green and withered over the spot where the great snow-soldier melted away; but the thoughts that came into those four boyish heads that day have kept on growing and gathering strength. How little they knew then, as they sang, and shouted, and whistled, and clapped the snow on here and there, that the fancies flitting to them from the white soldier would never leave them again! that while they were busily shaping his body, head, and arms to their satisfaction, he was quietly shaping *them*, actually molding their careers!

Neither did haughty Milly Scott imagine, as she walked by in her best clothes, that the snow-man would quite change her ways of thinking and acting; nor did little Ben, her brother, have any idea that the same shining white soldier would make him a prisoner for six weeks— not he. Yet these things all came to pass.

To-day, Sydney Burton (I do not give you his real name) is a sculptor in Rome; his brother, Colonel William Burton, is stationed somewhere on our Western frontier; Charley Green is soon to be made professor of chemistry in one of our Northern colleges; and solemn Hal McDougal is studying hard in the French Institute of Surgery.

As for Master Ben Scott and his sister Milly, perhaps I should have told you about them sooner in the story.

Poor Milly! She was not a bad-hearted girl, but she was very proud, and often blind to the feelings of others. She cared more for her fine clothes, her fancy boots, her wavy hair, than for anything else in the world, except her mother and father and little Ben. She disliked plain, unfashionable people exceedingly; and as for the really poor and ragged, they seemed to her too disagreeable to be thought of for an instant. She always avoided the wretched places where they lived, and never seemed to suspect that the little children whom Christ blessed were not all dressed in fine garments.

On this particular day, she had seen a child tumble over

a big frozen lump on the road, and when Ben tried to run toward it, she had pulled him back, saying:

"Stop, Benny! Don't touch the dirty little creature! Let her alone — she 'll stop crying in a minute."

"I wish I could give her a pair of shoes," Ben had said; "her feet look so cold!"

"Oh! poor people like her don't feel the cold. They are used to going barefoot," Milly had answered, still hurrying him on.

They ended their homeward walk in silence. Benny was feeling sorry for the very shabby and unhappy little girl, and Milly was trying not to blame herself, or at least to forget that pitiful little face by saying to herself: "It 's nothing to me, anyway."

That night, long after everybody was asleep, the snow-soldier came to Milly.

She was frightened at seeing him standing near her, but, somehow, she could n't call out or make any noise.

"Get up!" he said sternly.

She obeyed him. And now comes the strangest part of the story. She was Milly still, and yet so light that she seemed to float beside him out of the room, and down the stairs, and through the front door, and straight to the wretched part of the city where the poor folks lived. There she saw men, women, and children huddled together on bare floors or heaps of straw and rags, with scarcely anything to cover their poor, shivering bodies. Whenever the snow-man put his head in at the windows and doors, they would shiver worse than before, and utter moans that made Milly tremble. In one place she saw a pale young woman, with a baby in her arms, crouching before an empty stove. A few ashes lay on the hearth, and these would light up a little whenever the mother blew upon them. As the snow-man rattled the broken window-sash, the poor woman cried bitterly, and tried to warm the baby by holding it against her breast; but Milly knew, by the pinched look of the thin baby-face, that it was dying of hunger and cold.

Other sights they saw that made Milly's heart ache as it never had ached before; and when she asked leave to go home and send blankets and coal and wood to all these poor creatures, he held her back, growling:

"Come on! Poor people like these don't feel the cold. They 're used to it."

This sounded so cruel, so heartless, that Milly drew back in horror. Then the snow-man vanished. Whether he floated off or melted away, as snow-men often do, she never knew. But one thing is quite certain: from that night Milly began to improve. One does not in a twinkling conquer habits of selfish indifference and gain a life of good deeds and kindly sympathy for others. But Milly did improve wonderfully; and she never again said: "Oh! poor folks don't feel the cold."

KITTY'S CANARY

KITTY IS REMINDED OF FLUFFY. (SEE PAGE 258.)

SUCH a pet as Fluffy became at first sight! Papa had bought him to cheer Kitty when she was recovering from a tedious fever, and it really seemed as if Fluffy understood all about it. He appeared hardly to care for himself at all, though a new bird in a strange house certainly must have lonely and uneasy feelings at first. Fluffy never had lived the free out-of-door life that birds of his kind always enjoy in the Canary Isles; but he had come from a beautiful, sunny shop where there were rows upon rows of cages, and all the birds living in them knew one another by note, and were sure of having plenty of everything to make them comfortable. Mr. Carr, their owner, knew how important it was that his singers should be well cared for, and he always gave them fresh food and water every day.

Whether some other little bird told him or not, or whether Fluffy heard Kitty softly sobbing because the doctor had said she must stay in the house for a week longer, nobody can say. I only know that as soon as Fluffy's cage was hung by the window in Kitty's room, the little fellow began to take an interest. Yes, really to take an interest.

Kitty said so. He hopped from one perch to another, twitched his head this way and that, glanced about him with his quick little black eyes, saw that Kitty was down-hearted, and straightway began to sing!

"Cheer up, Kitty," he seemed to say. "I 'm here. Listen!" And then a trill, so sweet and soft and cheery, floated around the room and through the open window that Kitty brightened up wonderfully. Everything seemed different to her in an instant. To be confined to the house for a few days longer was not so bad, after all; and to be well enough to sit up and watch Fluffy, why, that was perfectly delightful! And what a dear, pretty little crea-ture he was—so light and soft and helpless, if you thought of him in one way; so brave and wise and wonderful, if you thought of him as he sat there cheering little Kitty! How he hopped, too: now to the floor of the cage, now to the perches, now to the seed-cup, stopping to sing at almost every turn! Kitty said it made her laugh to think how she would feel if she were to jump down to the kitchen, up to the roof, out in the garden, in at the window, all in a minute.

But was n't he tired? Did n't he want something more to eat? Would sugar hurt him? Was it safe to give him orange-peel? Did n't he need more gravel? More water? More anything? And if he did n't now, would n't he very soon? Kitty asked these questions of herself and those around her again and again. Her mother laughingly told her that as Mr. Warbler would need to be attended to every single day, he would be troublesome enough after a while. And Kitty hoped he would. It would be so nice to take care of the dear little fellow. Hey, Fluffy? So it would.   And all the time Fluffy kept on· singing, as if to say:

"Yes, Kitty, you look out for me, I 'll look out for you, and we 'll get on finely; so we will.

"This is a nice house, Kitty," his song seemed to say, when, after a while, he and the little girl were left alone together; "a very nice house. Pleasant window too, sunny and fine; pretty curtains, white as clouds, and thin as mist. *Kitty, Kitty, Kitty, Kitty, Kit—tee-e-e!* I like the way the wind lifts them. Don't you? Don't you? Every one 's so good to you, Kitty—Mama, Papa, Uncle Will, and all. Soon you can go out and play. Hey, Kitty? Eh—*Kitty, Kitty, Kitty, Kitty, Kitty, Kit, Kit—tee-e-e-e!*"

It all sounded so plain to Kitty, that, somehow, there was nothing strange in it. Why should n't dear little Fluffy say just such things to her when really her own heart was saying the same to him? She felt this all the while as she leaned back in the big easy-chair. It was a kind of duet between herself and Fluffy, growing softer and sweeter, sweeter and softer, every minute. Then when he happened to give an extra loud note of joy, she would rouse herself with a start and revel again in the delight of having a dear little canary-bird like Fluffy to love and care for.

The little fellow did not miss the bird-colony at Mr. Carr's, in the least. His new cage was large and pretty, and Kitty, who kept it in perfect order "all herself," was only too happy to attend to his every need. Even after she became able to go out and sit in the sunshine, she often would look up at the house and wave her hand

17

to Fluffy, or try to whistle to him as he merrily hopped about in his gilded cage.

But sometimes, as Kitty grew stronger and her little playmates began to call for her, right after breakfast, to join in this or that sport, she would fly out to them, actually neglecting to give Fluffy fresh seed and water. His cage hung out on the upper veranda now.

"An hour or so can't make any difference," she would say to herself,—"he 's all right"; and poor Fluffy would have to wait for her till after school.

How it came about, Kitty could n't tell. But, somehow, in meeting the girls again, and racing through the fields with them, and studying her lessons, and going out driving with Uncle Will, and doing all sorts of pleasant things, time slipped by; until one day, as she sat resting on the low stone fence in her father's orchard, watching a pair of busy birds flitting about among the branches of a stunted little tree, she wondered why they did not seek pleasanter quarters,—and then she suddenly thought of Fluffy!

With a quick pang of remorse and fright, Kitty sprang to the ground. She ran to the place where the cage hung. The water-cup was empty, the feed-cup empty—nothing but a few dried seed-husks scattered about. Fluffy was there, silent and alone, sitting on the lowest perch, and looking oh, so grieved!

"Fluffy! Fluffy!" sobbed Kitty, "here I am! I—I forgot you, Fluffy—but don't die!" and she started to get him something to eat.

But he already had fallen from his perch. With a cry Kitty tore open the little wire door, and, taking him in her hand, felt that he was still alive. He did not open his eyes, but when she moistened his bill with water, and sprinkled him, and laid him down on the sunny grass,— now feeding him drop by drop with sweetened water,— he stirred feebly; then he sank back.

"Mama, mama!" she called loudly, "come quick — Fluffy 's dying!"

But her mother had gone to the village with a friend. Their nearest neighbor, Mrs. Scott, came to the window; and Kitty called to her.

"Oh, Mrs. Scott! You have canaries. Do, please, tell me what to do for Fluffy! I forgot him, and he 's starved."

"Oh, you child!" exclaimed the neighbor, and in a few minutes (though it seemed a very long while to Kitty) she was kneeling beside the little girl, bending over Fluffy. She had a sheet of soft cotton in her hand. Tenderly and lightly folding the bird in it, she rose, and, pitying and comforting him as only a bird-lover could, she hastened home with the little sufferer—hardly noticing Kitty, except to repeat reproachfully, now and then, "Oh, you child! you child!"

"Can you do anything? Can you, Mrs. Scott?" pleaded Kitty, following her on a run.

"We 'll see. Oh, the poor little fellow!" said the neighbor, as they entered her cottage.

Did Fluffy live?

Well, well—you should have seen him a week or two later in his cage, jumping from perch to perch, on the floor, up to the seed-cup and down again, snapping the seeds hither and thither, and singing: "Kitty, Kitty, here we are! sweet and sunny; lovely, is n't it? Kitty! Kitty! Kitty! Here we are! Here we are!"

"Oh, you little sweetness!" cried Kitty, clasping her hands with joy. "I 'll never, never, *never* neglect you again! Mama says she 'll try me once more."

"Kitty, Kit-Kit-Kittee—ee-ee!" sang Fluffy.

GRANDMOTHER

GRANDMOTHER'S AFTERNOON NAP.

ONE fine October afternoon some years ago, my sister and I, happening to be in Germantown, that beautiful suburb of Philadelphia, went to call upon our well-remembered classmate Elsie G——. We found her and her two sisters, Helen and Mary, at home in the sunny, quaintly windowed living-room—and three very lovely girls they were. After they and their grandmother had given us a hearty welcome, Elsie said:

"Girls, Grandmother was just going to tell us something about Patty Burlock, as you came in. Would n't you like to hear it?"

We assured her that we should be delighted,—and Grandmama, after a little coaxing, began:

"It is only a simple incident that came to my mind a few moments back, hardly worth telling to an audience of five. It occurred at a church wedding that I attended eighteen—dear me! twenty-two years ago. I knew the bride and Patty too, as I was telling the children" (here, Grandmama looked beamingly at Helen, Elsie, and Mary). "Well, the long and short of it is, little Patty did speak right out loud in the middle of the ceremony.

"But if the minister had asked any other question than the one he did, it never would have happened.

"Or if it had been on any other day than that one particular day, it would n't have happened.

"If any other little boy in the whole wide universe excepting Robby Burlock had been with Patty, it never would have happened," she went on, with a playful nod.

"And I need n't tell you if it had been two strangers standing before the altar, instead of their sister Jessie and Herbert Norris, it never could have happened.

"But it *did* happen, for all that.

"If any one here present, said the minister, looking kindly upon the sweet bride with the brave young man beside her, and then glancing calmly over the little churchful of wedding guests, knows of any reason why this man and this woman should not be joined together in the holy bonds of matrimony, let him speak now, or,—

"'What 's all that?' whispered Robby, in great scorn, to Patty. 'I guess he does n't know. There ain't any bounds of materony about it.'

"That was enough. Young as he was, Robby was her oracle. Up jumped Patty, anxious to set things right, and determined that the wedding should go on, now that Sister Jessie had on her white dress and orange-flowers and lovely veil.

"'I do!' she called out in a sweet, resolute voice, as she held up a warning finger. 'I do. Please wait, Mr. Minister. There ain't any materony about it at all. They came on purpose to be married!'

"'O' course they did!' muttered Robby, distinctly.

"Everybody stared at Patty. It was a dreadful moment,
as you may believe, but the wedding went on all the same.

"And Patty and Robby, content and unabashed, were
among the very first to kiss the bride."

We all laughed heartily as the old lady ended her story, and she laughed with us.

"It so happened," she added, "that I was seated quite near the children, and I heard the whole thing. Their parents were with them, but were separated from them by Robby's little hat and coat, and Patty's big Leghorn hat, which lay on the seat.

"By the way, did n't one of you young folks tell me a while ago that Patty Burlock herself is going to be married next week?"

"Yes, indeed, Grandmother. We have cards for the wedding—and you must go, too."

"Not I, my dears. Grandma 's getting a little too stiff in her old age to be ambling to weddings and such things— but your young eyes will see it all, and you 'll tell me all about it."

The pleasant old lady leaned back in her rocker with so happy and satisfied an air as she said this, that, later, when Elsie, my sister, and I were sauntering through the grounds toward the summer-house, I could not help saying to our young hostess: "How changed your grandmother is! and for the better; she used to be so very quiet and grave. And how charmingly she told that little story!"

A peculiar expression crossed Elsie's face, as though the remark had given her both pain and pleasure. Then she replied, as she led the way into the crimson-vined summer-house:

"Yes, Grandmother has changed. So have we, for that matter. Come in and sit down a moment. I 'll tell you how it all came about:

" For a long time I did not understand it at all. I thought that, because grandmothers often were feeble and old-fashioned, they could never really feel as we children do; that they needed no particular notice or enjoyment, for it was their nature to sit in rocking-chairs and knit. They seemed quite different from the rest of the world, and not to be especially thought about; that is, by girls who were as full of merry plans as we were.

" Grandmother had lived with us of late years, as father is her only son. We had a vague idea that she helped Mother mend the clothes, and knitted Father's woolen stockings, besides some pairs for our church society. We were supposed to love her, of course, and we were never openly rude, for indeed we had been taught to be polite to all aged persons. As for Grandmother, she was one of those peaceful souls who never make any trouble, but just go on in their own way so quietly that you hardly know they are in the house. Mother sat with her sometimes, but we girls, in our gay, busy pursuits, rarely thought of such a thing. She seemed to have no part in our existence.

" It went on so for some time, till one day I happened at sundown to go into the sitting-room, and there sat Grandmother, alone. She had fallen asleep in her chair by the window. The sun was just sinking out of sight, casting a ruddy glow of light into the room, and in this glow I saw Grandmother — saw her really for the first time in my life !

" She had been reading her Bible, and then, as if there had been no need of reading more, since its treasure already lay shining in her soul, she had turned the book over upon her lap and leaned back to enjoy the evening.

"I saw it all in a moment,— her gentleness, her patience, her holiness. Then, while her love and beautiful dignity seemed to fold about me like a bright cloud, the sweet every-day lines in her face told me a secret,— that even then in the wonderful sunset of life she was, oh, how human! So human that she missed old faces and old scenes; so human that she needed a share of what God was giving us,— friends, home interests, little surprises and expectations, loving offices, and, above all, a recognition in the details of our fresh young lives.

"Girls, when Grandmother woke up, she found us all three stealing softly into the room; for I had told my sisters about it, and we all had talked it over. Mary only kissed her and asked if she had been having a good nap; Susie lifted her ball of yarn off the carpet, where it had rolled, and began to wind it, all the while telling her a pleasant bit of news about one of the school-girls; and I —well, I knelt down at Grandmother's feet and, just as I was going to cry, I gave her knees a good hard hug, and told her she was a darling.

"That's all, girls. Grandmother *is* different. And it's been different with us too ever since that day when she fell asleep by the window. Instead of our waking her, you see, she really wakened us."

TWO MAY-QUEENS

"AT THE KINDERGARTEN, THE CHILDREN RUSHED TO THE DOOR AND WINDOWS."

ONCE, not very long ago, and in a place not very far off, a ragged little lame girl sat upon a stone in the doorway of a poor hut, saying softly to herself:

"April showers bring forth May-flowers."

"They do, do they?" screeched a sharp voice from within. "I'll May-flowers you, if you don't look out! What you settin' out there for, Lerviny, and them clothes a-getting cold in the pail?"

"I'm a-lettin' 'em soak," answered the lame child gently, without looking up.

"You be, be you? Well, just you take yerself off of that, and come here to yer work. There's them collars all got to be starched."

Laviny, taking her rough little crutch, rose as quickly as she could, and, entering the dingy room, worked her way among tubs and broken chairs to an old pine table that held a pan of hot starch and a number of dry collars tied in a ragged towel.

"Can't I take 'em out in the sun, Aunt? I can't half see to do 'em in here."

Her aunt, who at the moment was bending over a tub-ful of steaming-hot clothes, was rubbing the schoolmaster's shirts so hard upon the washboard that she did not hear all that Laviny said. She saw the child's movement toward the door, however, and checked her with an impatient "No; stay where you be."

For a while after that, the only sounds in the cheerless room were the soft skish, s-k-ish of the starch under Laviny's thin little palms and her aunt's heavy rub, rub, rub upon the washboard.

Did the aunt hate little Laviny? Not she. Eliza Green was only rough, quick-tempered, and tired. If she thought about her conduct at all, she thought only that she was doing her duty in not letting the child "gad about outdoors" and in "puttin' a stop to the lazy ways she was a-getting into." Laviny, or Lavinia, was the orphan child of this washerwoman's sister, and it evidently was a settled matter somewhere far in the depths of the poor woman's dull, neglected heart that "so long as there was a day's washing to be found, or a crust or a smitch left, the poor little creetur should n't want for food and shelter; no, nor for careful trainin'." Presently, Laviny, squeezing a collar very hard and letting the starch ooze slowly through her fingers, looked wistfully toward the open doorway. Some white clouds were floating by in the distance.

"What 's got into yer, Lerviny? I 'll give yer somethin' to stare at if you don't take your eyes off that there sky."

(Only the day before, Eliza Green had told her friend Mrs. Delany, who lived in the shanty beyond, that that queer look of Laviny's always gave her "a crawl — like as if she was goin' to be took away from me, you know." But she did not say this to Laviny.)

"Why, Aunt," answered the little girl, in her sweet, patient voice, "I was only wondering about Miss Du-plaine's May-pole. Did n't you hear how Miss Duplaine's little girl 's going to be a May-queen? They 're going to have a great high pole, oh! ever so high! all hung full of flowers, and Miss Lotty 's a-going to have on her lovely white frock and loads of flowers around her head!"

"How d' yer know?"

"Why, I heard 'em talkin' about it when Jake Delany and me went last night to take home Miss Duplaine's clean clothes."

"Much *you* took home Miss Duplaine's clothes!"

"Well, I went with Jake, anyhow, an' I love him—he 's so good about carryin' me when I 'm tired."

"Lerviny! *Now*, see you looking so again! Let that there sky be! If you don't stop that way of lookin' up smilin' at the clouds, I 'll be after you, so I will."

"I was only thinkin' how good Jake is. And, Oh, Aunt! you ought to see the throne!"

The aunt gave a jump. "*What* throne, you on'arthly child, you?"

"Why, the one that 's for dear little Miss Lotty Du-plaine. It 's all made up pretty and green, and to-day she 's going to sit on it for Queen of May, and have a whole bushel o' flowers all throwed over her!"

"Sakes! what goin's-on them rich folks do have! I don't see no sense into it."

"Oh, Aunt Lizer! *I* do!"

Just then they heard a sound of mingled shouts and laughter and the tramping of little feet.

18

"Jake! Jake! Jake Delany!" screamed the chorus.

"What 's a-wantin'?" shouted back a gruff voice from the Delany shanty, which, with its low roof (like an old hat) slouching over its clear windows, stood quite near.

"Oh! we want you to come help us get some apple-blossoms. Come quick! we can't reach."

Laviny ran to the door and the aunt followed briskly. It was just noon. Jake Delany, Mrs. Delany's great, good-natured son, was shuffling his way toward Eliza Green's hut, and right outside, close to the very door-step, pressed a troop of happy, soiled, ragged, laughing children—and all carrying flowers! The girls had them in their aprons; the boys, bareheaded, held them in their hats and caps. One girl had a pailful of grass and dandelions, and a chubby little fellow, with red hair, held an old cracked pitcher full of blossoms and sprays of willow.

At the kindergarten up the village street the children rushed to the door and windows eager to see what was happening.

And nearer still, Mrs. Delany's little girl—younger than Jake—stood gazing wistfully at the merry crowd.

"Come along, Ma-ri-er," shouted some one; "we 're going to have lots of fun!"

"I can't," Maria called back. "The children are kind of ailin' and Ma can't spare me. I 've got to stay home with them."

"Hallo, Laviny!" shouted half a dozen; "we 're going to be needin' you soon."

"Needin' me?" almost screamed Laviny, her face sparkling with delight and astonishment. "Why, what for?"

"We 're going to keep May," answered the biggest girl, speaking for all, "and we 're going to make *you* Queen."

"I CAN'T. MA CAN'T SPARE ME."

"Oh! oh! oh!" said Laviny, clasping her hands. "And have flowers throwed all over me?"

"Yes," said the big girl, "and we 're goin' to crown you beautiful, and we 're goin' to fix a wand for you like Miss

Lotty's. We 've all been up to look through the bushes at her. My! it 's splendid!"

"She looks like a angel," put in one of the little girls, "with the loveliest white shoes and—"

"Ho!" interrupted another scornfully. "They don't have no shoes on angels."

"How you know?"

"'Cause I seed a pictyer of 'em. Ain't yer smart!"

"She had the elegantest ribbons onto her back, too, Laviny," spoke the big girl again. "But they took her right indoors. 'Fraid of her bein' so thin-dressed, I guess. Ready, Laviny? We want you right off."

"Where we going?" asked Laviny, all in a glow.

"Why, where we 've been fixin' the things, to be sure. Jake and Charley and Pete 'll have the blossoms all tied to the pole 'fore we get there. His daddy's long rake-handle makes a splendid one."

"*Do* let me go—please do," said Laviny, turning suddenly to her aunt. "Oh, can't I?"

"Why, what 's got inter yer, Laviny?" said the aunt, sharply; "anybody 'd think I was a bear to hear you go on. You hain't got a clean smitch on you, but never mind; go get your cape, it may blow up colder bimeby. Some o' you 'll have to help her 'long a little," she added, turning to the children, as Laviny went back into the shanty; "the poor child 's too much of a cripple to be May what-you-call-it."

"Oh! no, she is n't," shouted two or three. "We 'll take care of her."

"We picked her out for that," added a little girl quickly, "and because she 's so pretty and good."

"She is that," said Eliza Green, with a queer shine in her eyes; then, changing her tone, "Here, you, Laviny, don't you know they 're a-waitin'? You ain't a-makin' that air cape, be yer? I never see such a child."

Laviny came stumbling out with her crutch only half under her arm. Her face was so flushed and happy-looking that Mrs. Green gave her a slap as she passed out.

"Oh! oh!" exclaimed one of the girls.

"That 's nothing," laughed Laviny; "that 's only her way o' kissin' me. Aunt 's real good. Maybe she 'll go with us if you ask her."

One of the girls ran into the shanty, but came quickly out again with, "She says what 's the washin' to do, she 'd like to know?"

Nobody stopped to answer the question, and now Jake and Charley and Pete came running toward them.

"*Up* for a ride, little missy, grunted Jake, as, suiting the action to the word, he lifted Laviny up to a secure seat on his great square shoulder. " Here we go!"

It was a beautiful procession, after all. Jake ahead with his sunburned cheek looking all the ruddier beside Laviny's sweet, pale face, Tom Tice with his pitcherful, Kitty Carr with her pailful, and all the rest following with laden aprons and caps—it was a procession of flowers led on by the lily-girl shining up in Jake's arms. At last they reached the May-ground. It was only two fields off from Mrs. Duplaine's elegant place. They could see Lotty's beautiful May-pole distinctly, with its fluttering ribbons and long festoons of flowers. What if their May-pole *was* only a rake planted in the ground and wreathed with

18*

daisies and dandelions!   What if the throne *was* made of an old tub and a stool sprinkled over with cut grass! Did n't they trim Laviny's crutch with violets and apple-blossoms?   Did n't they crown her with a beautiful wreath?   Did n't they throw nearly a bushel of grass and flowers at her feet?   And did n't the biggest girl walk up to her, and with a funny little bob of a courtesy read these lines, written by Jake on a piece of wrapping-paper?—

> "Laviny Green,
>   You are our May-Queen."

That night, two little sisters, nestling in their straw bed on the floor, talked over the events of the day.

"*Was* n't Laviny sweet?" said one.   "I do think she 's feelin' real happy now, if she *is* lame!   It 's dreadful hard to have to walk crooked, ain't it?"

"Bet it is!   But I 'm glad we made her Queen o' May," said the other.

LITTLE HAL'S RICHES

LITTLE HAL'S RICHES

ONE day our little Hal was invited to spend the afternoon with his young playmate Johnny Lewis. Johnny's mother had died when he was a baby, but his father was still living. Johnny was an only child, and he dwelt in a fine house, and on Sundays rode to church in the grandest carriage to be met with in all the country round. He had a great many toys, and a *real* watch that would go all day and every day without stopping; and as for candies and cakes, why! the physician who attended the family said that Johnny had enough of such things given him to supply a whole regiment of little boys. He was a funny doctor, and liked to make droll speeches; but, for all that, he would often shake his head very gravely when he felt his little patient's pulse; then he would look sternly at the big gold watch which he held in his hand while counting Johnny's pulse-beats, and mutter, "Too many good things are bad things for youngsters." Johnny would try for a while to puzzle out the strange sentence, but as he was ill on these occasions, he would soon give up the attempt

281

in despair, and close his eyes, longing to get well, so that he might eat plumcake and popcorn balls again.

But Johnny was not always sick; and, as I said before, he had many beautiful things. So, of course, this visit promised Master Hal a world of enjoyment. But, alas! when the poor little fellow returned home in the afternoon, his brow was clouded, and he had a dismal look in his blue eyes, and the least bit of a pout on his cherry lips.

Something was wrong, I knew, and at last Hal gave it words.

"Mother, Johnny has money in *both* his pockets!"

"Has he, dear?"

"Yes; and he says he could get ever so much more, if he wanted it."

"Well, now, that makes it very pleasant for Johnny," I returned cheerfully, as a reply evidently was expected. "Very pleasant; don't you think so?"

"Yes, only —"

"Only *what*, Hal?"

"Why, he has a big pop-gun and a gold watch and a hobby-horse, and lots of things." And Hal looked up into my face with a disconsolate, doleful stare.

"Well, my boy, what of that?"

"Nothing, Mother," and the telltale tears sprang to his eyes, "only I think we 're very poor, are n't we?"

"No indeed, Hal, dear; we are very far from being poor. But we are not so rich as Mr. Lewis's family, if that is what you mean."

"Oh, Mother!" insisted the little fellow, "I do think we 're very poor; anyhow *I* am!"

"Oh, Hal!" I exclaimed reproachfully.

"Yes, ma'am, I *am*," he sobbed; "I have n't anything at all scarcely — I mean anything that 's worth money — except things to eat and wear, and I 'd have to have them anyway."

"*Have* to have them?" I echoed, at the same time laying my book upon the couch on which we were sitting, and preparing to reason with the young gentleman on this point; "do you not know, my son — "

Just then Uncle Ben called out from the next room, where he had been reading his newspaper, "What 's the matter with the little man? Come in here, my boy."

"Hal," said he solemnly, nodding slyly to me by way of showing that he had overheard our conversation, "you know I 'm a doctor, and if you 'll give me a chance to try some experiments you can earn a lot of money."

"Can I?" asked Hal, looking up quickly through his tears; "I 'd like that ever so much; but what is a 'speriment, Uncle?"

"An experiment," said his uncle, "is a trial, a way of finding out things. If you want to find out what will happen when sugar is put into water, you simply try the experiment of putting a lump into this tumbler, so, and you 'll find out that the sugar 'll melt and the water will become sweet. If you should put slices of lemon into the water, what would happen?"

"The water would be sour," replied Hal, promptly.

"Yes, sir; you 're right," said his uncle. "So much for experiment. Now for business.

"I want to find out something about eyes; so, if you 'll

let me have yours, I'll give you ten dollars apiece for them."

"For my eyes!" exclaimed Hal, astonished almost out of his wits.

"Yes," resumed Uncle Ben, quietly, "for your eyes. I promise not to hurt you a particle. Only you could n't see out of them any more. Come, sir! ten dollars apiece, cash down. What do you say?"

"Give you my eyes, Uncle! Why, I 'd be blind!" cried Hal, looking wild at the very thought. "For two ten dollars? I think not!" and the startled little fellow shook his head defiantly.

"Well, thirty;—forty;—fifty;—a hundred dollars, then?" but Hal shook his head at every offer.

"No, sir! I would n't let you for a thousand dollars. Why, what could I do without my eyes? I could n't see Mother, nor the baby, nor the flowers, nor the horses, nor anything," added Hal, waxing warmer.

"I 'll give you five thousand!" urged Uncle Ben, taking a roll of bank-notes out of his pocket. Poor little Hal, standing at a respectful distance, shouted that he never would do any such thing.

"Very well," continued his uncle, with a serious, businesslike air, at the same time writing down something in his note-book, "I can't afford to give you more than five thousand dollars, Hal; so I shall have to do without the eyes; but," he added, "I 'll tell you what I will do: I 'll give you twenty dollars if you will let me put a few drops out of this bottle into your ears. It will not hurt, but it will make you deaf. I want to try some experiments with deafness, you see. Come now. Here are the twenty dollars all ready for you."

"Make me deaf!" shouted Hal, without even looking at the money temptingly displayed upon the table. "I guess you won't do that either. Why, I could n't hear a word if I was deaf, could I?"

"Probably not," replied Uncle Ben, dryly. So, of course, Hal refused again. He would never give up his hearing, he said,—"No, not for three thousand dollars!"

Uncle Ben made another note in his book, and then came out with prodigious bids for Hal's "voice," for his "right arm," then "left arm," "hands," "just one leg," "feet," and so on, finally ending with an offer of ten thousand dollars for "Mother" and five thousand for "the baby."

To all of these offers, however, Hal shook his head, his eyes flashing, and exclamations of surprise and indignation bursting from his lips. At last Uncle Ben said he must give up his experiments, for the young man's prices were entirely too high.

"Ha-ha!" laughed Hal exultingly, and he folded his arms and looked as if to say, "I'd like to see the man who could pay them!"

"Why, Hal, look at this!" exclaimed Uncle Ben, peering into his note-book, "here is a big addition sum; come, help me do it."

Hal looked into the book, and there, surely enough, were all the figures. Uncle Ben read the list aloud:

"Eyes, $5000; ears, $3000; voice, $2000; right arm, $4000; left arm, $4000; hands, $2000; one leg, $4000; feet, $3000; Mother, $10,000; Baby, $5000."

He added the numbers together, and they amounted in all to forty-two thousand dollars.

"There, Hal," said Uncle Ben, "don't you think you are foolish not to take to some of my offers?"

"No, sir, I don't," answered Hal resolutely.

"Then," said Uncle Ben, "you talk of being *poor*, and by your own showing you have treasures that you 'll not take forty-two thousand dollars for. What do you say to that?"

Hal did n't know exactly what to say; so he laughed and blushed for a second, and then with shining eyes exclaimed:

"Why, I 'm awful rich! all of us — you and Mama and everybody! but Uncle —"

"Well, sir?"

"Why, Johnny Lewis has got 'em too — besides the gold watch and the money in his pockets and everything!"

"My stars!" cried Uncle Ben in great surprise — for, to tell the truth, he *was* a little taken aback (as he afterward confessed to me, in confidence)—" Well, what 's going to be done about it?"

"Nothing," said Hal, rosy with joy as he strode about, proud of his legs, his muscle, and all his possessions — "It 's all right — everybody 's rich enough after they find it out."

"Right you are," said Uncle Ben, quietly slipping from the room.

ONLY A ROSE

THE SISTERS.

ONLY A ROSE

A TRUE STORY

ONE day, many years ago, Mother summoned all of us children—Marie, Gertrude, and me—to her sitting-room, and made an announcement.

"Children," said she, "I am going to the country with your father, to remain a week."

Dear me! how our hearts sank!

"Miss Ellis will remain at home with you," continued Mother, "and I trust she will have a pleasant account to give me on my return. She will tell me, I think, Marie, that you have been a kind, faithful girl, keeping good watch over your younger sisters." (Marie smiled, though her eyes were fast filling with tears.) "That you, Lilly, have been quite steady, getting into no mischief whatever." (I was the wild one of the household.) "And that you, my little Rosebud" (kissing Gertrude), "have obeyed her in everything like a little lady."

When Mother ceased speaking, she put her arms round us, and looked into our faces to see what answers she

19   289

could find there. Marie met her glance in a way that, I know, satisfied Mother. I kissed her, and inwardly resolved that I would n't go to the sugar-bowl all the while she was gone; no, not once! And little Gertrude, who was not four years old, looked up and shook her head saucily as if to say, " I 'll think about it, Mother. My conduct will depend entirely upon what turns up."

This is the way Gertrude *looked*, I say ; but, if the truth could be known, we probably would find that she had already forgotten Mother's words, and just shook her head because we all were watching her.

Mother talked with us a little longer, and then sent down-stairs for our governess. This was Miss Ellis, a dear, good lady, who was almost as kind as Mother. We loved her very much, and when she looked brightly at us and said, " Oh, I am sure they all will be very good and obedient while Mama is gone," we echoed her words from the depths of our saddened little hearts.

It was interesting enough to see Miss Ellis put all the wonderful things into the trunk — gloves, laces, the fan that sparkled when you shook it, the little pink shawl trimmed with swans' down, that Mother used to throw around her shoulders when she " dressed up "; the funny work-bag that shut by pulling two strings ; and the beautiful chintz dress with birds flying all over it. But our hour of enjoyment was short. When the trunk was locked, strapped, and placed in the hall ; when Father, who came home to dinner that day, told Miss Ellis just how to send for them in case anything should happen ; and when, above all, Father and Mother kissed us for " good-by " and were really going, and we sobbing ones (after a whispered hint from Miss Ellis) were wishing them "a very hap-ap-py time," we felt that nothing more dreadful had ever happened to three poor, forsaken children.

As soon as the carriage rolled away, and Miss Ellis closed the street door, Marie just leaned her back against it and cried; I sat down on the mat, forgetting my clean white dress, and sobbed aloud; and little Gerty cried because Marie and I did. I do believe, if some fairy had made my new wax doll walk down-stairs at that moment, and take a seat on my lap, I should n't have noticed it much; or if the sugar-barrel had come bumping up the kitchen stairs, and rolled past me, spilling sugar all the way, I really could not have taken any for at least two minutes, I was so wretched.

Seven days! Only to think of it! Why, a day appeared nearly as long to me then as a month does now, and a week without Mother seemed too cruel to think of—almost as dreary as going through a dark tunnel fifty miles long. I had yet to learn that to sit down and cry over such a trouble was one of the silliest things in the world. Miss Ellis told us so then, and tried to comfort us, but we hardly heeded her. Indeed, we might have sobbed there for an hour longer, if a well-known voice had not called us, from the foot of the kitchen stairs:

"Doan be cryin' dar, chillen! Come down ter ole Lizer. I 'm a-gwine ter make cookies!"

Those words sent a ray of bright sunshine through the lonely hall, I can tell you! Marie gave her eyes one or two final rubs with her apron; Gerty clapped her hands and ran to "Lizer"; and I rose and walked slowly down the hall, letting my lips stick out pretty far, so as to feel miserable as long as possible.

"Jump, dearie!" we heard the cheerful voice say to Gerty, who loved, when nearly at the bottom of the stairs, to leap into Eliza's arms. "Jump-a-daisy! doan be afeard! Ole Lizer 'll ketch yer!"

In another moment, Marie and I rushed joyfully into the kitchen, exclaiming, "Will you bake us a bogie man, Eliza? Will you bake us a bogie man?"

"Course I will, honey; but you muss all be circumspectious, now. Can't hab no fussin' in dis yere kitchum."

We were so well accustomed to this command, that it produced but little effect upon us. I was upon the kitchen table "as quick as a wink," and Gerty ran up and down the well-scrubbed floor, laughing and shouting with delight. Meanwhile, Eliza moved slowly and steadily about the large kitchen, from pantry to table, from table to dresser, her shining brown face beaming with kindness, yet grand to our eyes with its look of importance; her great plump form arrayed in a dark calico gown, covered with the cleanest of check aprons; a bright plaid kerchief tied about her head; another folded over her bosom. I can hear her soft, heavy tread yet as it sounded that day while she placed the sugar, eggs, butter, dishes, and other articles upon the kitchen table. At last came the white flour-pail, crowned with a big sieve, and then I knew that my time to dismount from the table had arrived. Eliza spoke even while I was scrambling down: "Get off of dar, Miss Lilly; can' hab no chillen cumberin' up dis yere table!"

Oh, what fun it was to see the butter and sugar, all lumpy and mottled when first stirred together, grow into a smooth golden paste under the strokes of her wooden spoon! to see the beaten eggs, like a little sea of foam, grow less and less in their fragrant bed! then the snow-like fall of flour, as with one hand she shook the sieve, while stirring briskly with the other! and, above all, to see the completed dough flatten out under the rolling-pin, all ready to be stamped into cookies! Marie, being the eldest, always had the privilege of stamping out a few with the tin cover of the little nutmeg-can; and, provided I had faithfully kept my fingers out of the cinnamon-box and not upset anything upon the table, I was sometimes allowed to test my skill too. As soon as the cookies were finished came the grand performance of bogie-baking. Such lovely men! One for Marie, one for Gerty, and one for me —all with arms thicker than their legs, and noses bigger than their feet; or, rather, they often developed these pe-culiarities after they were put into the oven. Two pieces of cloves for eyes, and a strip of citron for the mouth, com-pleted their charms. Soon the oven was quite filled. The kitchen grew more and more delightful with the odor of baking cookies, and we children clustered together on the great window-bench, while Eliza made the kitchen, as she said, look "a leetle scrumptuous" again.

When we went up-stairs, Miss Ellis let us play in the nursery until tea-time; so the afternoon passed away pleas-antly enough, though we felt lonely at supper, notwith-standing the cookies and our beautiful little bogies. It seemed doleful to close our eyes that night without

19*

Mother's "good night" kiss; but Miss Ellis allowed **Marie** and me to pommel each other with the pillows for a **while** before going to sleep, and that was a great consolation.

I cannot recall much of the second day of Father's and Mother's absence. Probably we were good and happy, or I should remember something about it, for clouds are apt to make stronger pictures on the memory than sunshine. Oh, yes; Henry Garnet came in from the country. He was Eliza's husband, or "ole man," **as** she called him, and he well knew that he was always welcome to a home with us for Eliza's sake. He was old and infirm, and would sit by the kitchen stove hour after hour, rising only when Eliza's cheerful voice said, "Here, ole man, just fotch me a skettle o' coal, if you ain't grow'd fast ter dat yar stool," or, "Here, ole man, just fotch in a pail of water, will yer?"

These little demands attended to, old Henry would sit down again and settle into his afternoon doze, leaning his head tenderly against the wooden mantel, and folding his hands before him, quite **sure** that "Lizer" would set him up straight, in case he "took to leanin' over too much to one side," as he often did. It **was** strange **to see** her pause in her busiest moments, and, walking toward the dozing old man, straighten his leaning form in the most businesslike way, never murmuring though she had to repeat the performance half a **dozen** times during his nap.

"Ah, Miss Ellis," she said, one day, "men *is* unhandy things ter hab aroun', specially in a kitchum; but den de old gem'man's had a hard time **bein'** knocked about in dis worl', an' while de **Lord** spares him, **ole Lizer** doan mind **de trouble.**"

Well, Henry came just before dinner, and the rest of the day is a blank in my mind; but the next morning stands out bright and clear. It was Sunday. After breakfast, Marie and I were dressed for church, and, while Miss Ellis was getting ready to go with us, we were all three allowed to walk a while in the garden. It was a plain city yard, with grassplot in the middle, bordered with a flower-bed with fine rose-bushes in each corner. During the past few days we had been watching the buds with great interest (for it was June), and now, to our great joy, we found three lovely new roses nestling amid the green. Our shouts of delight brought Miss Ellis to the window.

After gently chiding us for making so much noise, Miss Ellis told us (especially Gerty) not on any account to pick the roses, for she wished the bush to look as beautiful as possible when our parents should return. Marie and I saw Gerty look wistfully up at the window, after Miss Ellis left it, and then walk slowly toward the bush. We almost *knew* that she meant to pick a rose (the very prettiest one of all) hanging within reach of her chubby hand. Either Marie or I could easily have prevented it; but Mother's wish was forgotten. Was Marie "keeping faithful watch over her sisters"? Was I "steady, keeping out of all mischief"? No! we both looked on—Marie indifferently, and I, filled with mischievous glee, thinking of "the time" Miss Ellis would make if Gerty should disobey her.

In a few moments the rose was pulled from its stem. While we were looking at it, Miss Ellis came to the door of the back piazza in plain sight of the blooming rose-bush, which was still stirring after its tussle with Gerty.

"Who picked that rose?" she asked sternly.

Gerty held the flower so tightly that it was all crushed; but none of us answered.

"Did *you* pick it, Gerty?" asked Miss Ellis, in a sorrowful tone.

"'Es; Gerty picked it," replied Gerty, backing toward us as she spoke.

"Then Gerty has been disobedient. Gerty must be punished."

The frightened little creature began to cry. Marie and I held our breaths. Miss Ellis took her up to one of the garret rooms; it had nothing in it but an old chair and a doll, which lay upon the floor. It was a gloomy room, with only one window, and that was so high up that we never could look out of it without climbing up on something.

Gerty sobbed bitterly when Miss Ellis told her, as they started for this room, that she must stay there alone for five minutes, and we felt half tempted to follow and rescue her by main force. But when we heard our governess shut the door of the lonely room, and walk away, we ran down into the front hall as fast as our legs could carry us.

It was now nearly church-time, the bells were ringing, and as we stood on the front stoop, waiting for Miss Ellis to join us, we saw the people walking quietly on their way to church. We felt sorry for Gerty, but tried to comfort ourselves with the secret falsehood that we could n't help it. "Pshaw!" I thought, "it was only a rose, after all; there's no harm done." "It was disobedience, too, and you should have saved your little sister from the act," whispered something within me; but I hushed the voice, and kept repeating as I stood there, "It was only a rose, anyhow."

By this time I felt sure that the "five minutes" must be nearly over, and was raising my eyes to the dormer windows of the garret, and feeling very sorry for the poor little prisoner, when suddenly I saw something spinning down through the air from the very top of the house—spinning, falling, nearer and nearer, until it struck the iron railing of the front piazza, and then fell heavily upon the stone pavement. Oh, it was Gerty! Gerty! our own darling little sister!

Eliza and old Henry came rushing up the front cellar steps. I remember his bent body; the gathering crowd; the quiet little form upon the pavement; the crimsoned arm; the screams and sobs of Marie, Miss Ellis, and Eliza; the momentary tumult and terror; then the awful hush when she was laid, still and white, upon the sofa. Would she ever open her eyes—ever speak to us again? The doctor shook his head when Miss Ellis looked imploringly into his face. She was frantic with grief, and Eliza, groaning and crying, dashed water upon Gerty's white face, without effect. The kind-hearted creature, even in her distress, had a word of sympathy for Miss Ellis.

"Ah, chile," she sobbed, "don't take on—don't take on—de Lord knows yer was tryin' to do right. Oh! if dose bressed little eyes would on'y look at ole Lizer jist once. If you'd on'y brought out de chair, Miss Ellis—but still it seemed out o' natur for de poor little creatur' to drag it to de winder all herself. Oh, doctor, doctor, *is* she killed? De Lord have mercy. *Is* she killed?"

Soon the surgeon arrived. After he had been with her for nearly an hour, set and bandaged the poor little arm, which was broken in two places, and with his assistant attended to her dreadful wounds and bruises, we were told that Gerty had opened her eyes and asked faintly for a drink of water. A messenger had gone on horseback to summon Father and Mother. He crossed the ferry to Long Island, and then, lashing his horse, never halted until he reached the farm-house where they were visiting. The horse bore him nobly, but fell dead a few moments after reaching the house. Gerty did not know Father and Mother when they came. She did not notice anything, but she was living, and that was more than they had dared hope for.

It was a terrible time. For weeks their little one hovered between life and death; but their prayers were answered. In course of time she grew stronger; new color bloomed in her cheek, and her pattering feet once more made music for the household. She lived, a bright, playful child, and not an invalid or cripple, as all had feared she would be; but never again did either Marie or I, while thinking upon all that happened on that sad June morning, dare say in our hearts, " It was only a rose."

LIMPETTY JACK

THE BOYS HELD MANY A CONSULTATION IN FRONT OF THE COUNTRY STORE.

But Master Phil was a self-willed little fellow, and he followed Limpetty Jack on the sly, slipping in and out among the low bushes and rocks, not showing himself till they were at the very mouth of the cave. All those thoughtless boys were hidden away in the cave, almost bursting with suppressed laughter, and waiting to see what Limpetty Jack would do when he should come upon the monster.

"You can't go in with me," whispered Limpetty Jack to Philly, when at last he discovered him just outside the entrance to the cave.

"But I *will*," insisted the child.

"We'll see," said Limpetty Jack, as, catching the boy in his arms, he waded into the water with him and set him down upon a great rock that reared its top out of the waves.

"Sit ye there like a good boy till I come back with the bag of gold," said Limpetty Jack. There was no danger of his being disobeyed, for, little as he was, Phil knew he must drown if he slid off of the rock. And if he should try it, who could hear him scream through all the wailing of the sea!

"*Now!*" said Limpetty Jack, as he entered the cave.

"My stars!" he cried faintly, as his astonished gaze fell upon the terrible figure squatted in the corner, "but the mermaids have a mighty queer taste in the way of husbands!"

Still he was too eager for his bag of gold to back out now.

"Good day, sir," said he, bowing as well as he could,

considering his wet legs and the trembling that suddenly came over him.

"Good day to you," croaked a strange voice. "I have brought you a bag of gold from my wife."

"Many thanks to her, I 'm sure, sir," faltered Limpetty Jack, bowing again, and stepping slowly forward inch by inch.

"But," roared the mermaid's husband, "you cannot have it for nothing. There must be a sacrifice. Get your fine dog Shag, and stand him on the great rock near by, in the sea, and when the waves wash him off and take him to my wife, the gold is yours."

Poor Jack's teeth chattered. Stupid though he was, he dearly loved Shag, and Shag loved him; but he could not bear to give up the gold.

"Your Mightiness," said he plaintively, "could n't ye think of some other sakeryfice?"

"Not another," bellowed the mermaid's husband, and a low rumbling sound seemed to spring up in the cave; but it was only those wicked jokers trying not to laugh. One of them had whispered to another:

"Now for it! Limpetty 's so scared he 'll never remember that Shag 's a swimmer!"

But with that ugly monster before him, the poor dull-witted fellow was ready to believe that any impossible thing might happen. Some other dreadful creature might appear from the depths and drag his beloved Shag down under the sea.

"Well, sir," said Limpetty Jack, after a little bewildered hesitation, "I have n't any too much sense. *That* I know as well as the best one. But I like my dog Shag too well to give him up for all the gold of the sea," and with a great sigh he turned to go away.

"Hold!" he cried, suddenly recollecting something. "I *did* leave behind me, on the great rock in the sea, a most beautiful boy. I did n't mind me to do it; but he would follow me against my will. So I set him there to keep him out of sight till I could meet your worship alone as I was told. Yes, he 's there — a most beautiful boy, your worship, the son of one Philigan McDerm—"

Oh! but you should have seen the monster spring to his feet, cast off his mask, and tear out of the cave, he and all the wicked jokers after him! Limpetty Jack ran too, and now he cared far more for finding poor little Phil than for all the gold that ever was seen.

The tide had risen fast, and nearly covered the great rock, and there on the very top, with the water close upon his tiny feet, stood frightened, screaming little Phil.

It seemed as if the waves—each greater than the one before it—must throw him off. They rushed into the sea. It was hard work;—but Limpetty Jack was first. The rising waters were knee-high — breast-high—chin-high; and all the while the waves were dashing them against the sharp rocks. The strongest of them drew back discouraged. Then all they could distinguish was Limpetty Jack's black head. They had seen the frantic little boy leap toward it as if Jack had called him, and then Phil McDermot, who had stood in the waves as if turned into stone, was thrown violently back upon the shore.

When he opened his eyes, there stood his little son beside

20

him, screaming with terror at the father's outlandish dress. The boys were crowding about Limpetty Jack, cheering him, shaking his hands, clapping his shoulders, and thanking him with full hearts. He seemed dazed at first; but after they had hurried him into the nearest house, and put dry clothes upon him, he asked for little Philly Mac, and wept with joy to know that the child was safe.

Strange to say, he seemed to brighten in his wits from that day. It might have been owing to the shock, or to his bravery in saving little Phil, or to the fact that people young and old at last thought of helping him. Certain it is, the boys were his friends. Never again did even · the most mischievous among them play any prank upon Limpetty Jack.

BUBBLES

BUBBLES

AS TOLD BY JOEL STACY

It is so long since it happened, my dears, that whenever I think about it, the youngest of my acquaintances fade quite out of sight; dear middle-aged faces grow rosy and youthful; Mary, my grave little wife, suddenly goes dancing down the garden path with a skipping-rope; our worn-out old Dobbin becomes a frisky colt; the tumbled-down affair yonder, behind the pile of brush, straightens itself into a trim, freshly-painted woodshed; and — well, the long and short of it is this: the memory of that day always carries me back to the time when I was a little boy.

You see, I sat on the porch blowing soap-bubbles. I remember it just as if it were yesterday. The roses were out and the wheelbarrow had a broken leg; the water in the well was low, and if you tried to climb up on the curb to look down into it you 'd have some one calling for you to "come away from there." But you could do what you pleased on the porch. It was so warm and sunny that Mother let me leave off my shoes as a matter of course. It seems to me that I can remember just how the hot boards felt to the soles of my tiny bare feet. Certainly I can recall how Rover looked, exactly — he has been dead these dozen years, poor fellow!

The lather must have been precisely right, for I know it worked beautifully. Such bubbles as I blew that morning! What colors they displayed! How lightly they sailed up into the clear air! Sometimes a little one with a bead at the end — a failure — would fall upon Rover's nose and burst so quickly that I could n't tell whether its bursting made him blink or his blinking made it burst. Sometimes a big one would float off in the sunlight and slowly settle upon the soft grass, where it would rock for an instant, then snap silently out of sight, leaving only a glistening drop behind. And sometimes — but here I must begin afresh.

The little girl who lived next door very soon came and leaned her bright head out of the window. A bubble had just started at the end of my pipe. I did n't look up; but I knew she was watching me, and so I blew and blew just as gently and steadily as I could, and the bubble grew bigger, bigger, bigger, until at last it almost touched my nose. Then it let go; and looking up at it, I saw in the beautiful ball first the blue sky, then perfect little apple-tree branches, then I saw the house, then the open window and the little girl!

This made me shout with joy. I called out, but the little girl was gone. Probably she had bobbed her head back into the room. It was just like little girls to do so, you know. Then I blew others, and knew she was watching me again; and, all of a sudden, Mother called me.

Well, I cannot remember much more about that summer. It seems to me that there were peaches, and that

Rover learned to draw a wagon; but I 'm not sure whether that happened just then or a year or two later.

The next thing that comes up is a school-room. I must have been a big boy by that time, for I remember having my pockets full of marbles; also I remember having a black eye on account of a fellow named Townley. (Townley is in the sugar business now.) Besides, I was in fractions, and, though I did n't care very much for study, I did n't wish *her* to think I was stupid. Who? Did n't I tell you? Why, a little girl who went to the same school,—a little girl in a pink calico dress and a white sunbonnet. She had a way of dropping her books on her way home from school, I remember, and we fellows used to jump for them so as to have the fun of handing them to her. Well, the way I used to try to get up head in the classes when she was there was astonishing. The other fellows tried to show off, too; but I knew by the way that she did n't ever notice me unless I spoke to her that she thought my bubble was the biggest. You see it was only blowing bubbles again, after all.

Well, time flew along, and at last war came. I was a stout fellow then ; Mother said I could go,—bless her brave heart!—and I went. The scenes, the horrors of that war! But we 'll not talk of them now. It 's enough to say that though I felt patriotic and all that, I specially wished to distinguish myself — well, I don't mind telling you in confidence — so that Somebody with brown, laughing eyes and a gentle voice would be almost as proud as Mother to see me coming back with honors.

Blowing bubbles again, you 'll observe.

"THERE SAT MY LITTLE MAN, AND IF THE YOUNG SCAMP WAS N'T BLOWING
BUBBLES!"

Once more time flew along. Why not? And again I found myself trying—this time to make money. The day, as I look back, is so close that the old faces put on their own look again, and the young acquaintances come to light once more, and Mary, my wife, no longer skipping down the garden path, sits at her little work-table sewing. Well, as I have said, this time I am trying to make money. There is great excitement in Wall street. Men are being made rich or poor in an hour. I have a good, steady clerkship, but a chance for blowing a great big, big bubble comes to me. I can see a happy face already looking up at me from its golden surface.

Other men have succeeded. She shall be rich now!

I blow and blow, and the bubble bursts! All gone,—gone in a flash,—the savings of years! Ruined!

I hurry home—though it is but the middle of the day. No one there. I sit down to think. Ruined? Not a bit of it. Have n't I health and honesty and strength? Have n't I Father and Mother and have n't I Mary and have n't I young Joe?

With this thought, and hearing our Ponto give a brisk questioning bark of attention, and Joe calling me, I stepped to the back window and looked out. Surely enough, there sat my little man, and if the young scamp was n't blowing bubbles! And, if you 'll believe me, the little girl next door was leaning out of the window watching him! Just then, Mary came in,—I mean just now, for the fact is I 'm writing about this very day. And both Mary and I think it is n't such a very dreadful thing, after all, to lose a few hundred dollars, for I have my clerkship yet, and I 'm determined never to speculate with my savings again. No, I 'm going to be a steady, faithful, hard-working fellow, and Mary and Mother and Joe and I are going to be just as comfortable and happy as birds—and—and—

You see, I am blowing this new bubble so slowly and cautiously in the sunlight that I know it will be all safe. And right in the heart of it I see Mary—Mary who has looked brightly up at me from every bubble that I have ever blown in all my life.

www.ingramcontent.com/pod-product-compliance
Lightning Source LLC
Chambersburg PA
CBHW060518030726
47498CB00004B/992